A

CHRISTMAS

VISITOR

A

CHRISTMAS

VISITOR

A Novel

David Saperstein
&
George Samerjan

•NOW A HALLMARK MOVIE•

RED SKY PRESENTS
NEW YORK

With James J. Rush

A CHRISTMAS GIFT

Non-Fiction

WOMAN IN THE YEAR 2000 (Editor –
Maggie Tripp)

OTHER BOOKS BY GEORGE SAMERJAN

LONG WAY HOME

FROM THE SHADOWS

HOME WITHOUT A FLAG (POEMS
WRITTEN IN VIETNAM DURING THE WAR
AND BACK IN THE WORLD)

ACKNOWLEDGEMENTS

Sara Camilli – Our super-agent who kept our Christmas dreams alive and revealed

Audrey LaFehr – Our editor who understood and kept the spirit of Christmas with us

Ivan Saperstein – Our high-powered, creative lawyer and advisor who always keeps our best interests, and our work, first and foremost

Micky Hyman – Our 21st Century publisher who knows how to bring a good story to the world

Jesse Sanchez – A true artist who captured the spirit of our story for the cover

For my wife Ellen, who has always encouraged and supported me throughout our life's passage.

David

For my wife, Joy whose partnership transcends the passage of our lives.

George

CONTENTS

CHAPTER ONE

A PRIVATE MOMENT

Each year brought a different perspective; like with changing seasons, the passage of time revealed different hues of color, from bright to muted, to bright again reflecting the loss he carried deep inside. The emptiness seemed to diminish, nor ease, though twelve years had passed.

The cold, threatening, November day had kept people indoors. As the crisp autumn night rapidly descended, the Town Square was deserted. George Boyajian stood motionless on the narrow, gray stone sidewalk that led to the town's War Memorial. His six foot, sixty year old frame was erect; shoulder square - the physique of a man twenty years younger. George's full head of brown hair gave no hint of age, though some grey flecks had begun to appear at his temples. Under his weathered leather jacket, and fleece-lined gloves, were powerful, sinewy arms and hands - the result of a life's work in the building trades. He was a master carpenter.

George Boyajian had, for the past twelve years, observed a private ritual on the night before the somber public assembly took place at the memorial. He moved forward down the walkway toward the five polished native granite columns which formed a circle of honor. Each column was fronted with a brass plaque. His heart pounded. A chill ran down his spine as he heard the rattle of the rope tapping against the hollow flagpole, and the crack of the American flag snapping briskly in the breeze above. It caused him to gaze up at the stars and stripes, illuminated against a brilliantly starry sky. The sound and image transcended time, stringing his memories of this place together like dark pearls in an endless necklace. He did not feel the chill wind. The acuity of his vision was almost surreal. He could see every broken blade of grass along the path, every stone, and every patch of earth - all fitting together in a sentient mosaic. George stopped again. It was 1966 and he was standing at attention in his fatigues, in Vietnam at a jungle base camp as the chaplain read the names of that week's fallen. In that far-away, long-ago place, he might well have been one of the names announced...names recorded on lists of wars - wars begun millennia ago with rosters of the dead in the millions. And still there was no end to them in sight.

His memory and reflection was but a momentary diversion. He walked on, wanting to be strong for John's sake. And that's why George Boyajian would come to this place the night before the annual ceremony - to inoculate himself against any public display of hurt and loss. His private emotions locked away while he performed his public duty.

"Oh dear God," George whispered inside himself. "My dear God..." Gathering courage, and remembering his pledge to honor John, he reverently walked into the circle of the five stone columns.

The names of deceased servicemen from New Chatham were displayed on the column's brass plaques. The Great War, the one they said was to end all wars, contained eight names; World War Two listed twenty soldiers, sailors, and marines who had fallen; five men had been killed in the Korean Conflict – a police action they called it; the Vietnam War plaque listed twelve men who had made the supreme sacrifice in South Vietnam, Laos, and Cambodia. George shook his head in somber disbelief at the number of souls his small town had offered to America. He paused briefly before the Vietnam plaque. It listed the names of his schoolmates and friends who had died in Vietnam. He knew them all. It still amazed George, after nearly four decades that his name was not engraved there. He was here, living and breathing. Yet part of him had been left behind, forever entwined in the souls of those who fell beside him.

The last plaque, memorializing the first Iraq War, contained only one name, his son, John Boyajian. He removed a small plastic baggie from his pocket. In it was a cloth he had partly dipped in Brasso. He gently rubbed the brass letters of John's name with the caustic fluid and then wiped it dry with the rest of the cloth.

"There you are, son. All spit and polish." George knelt. First with his eyes, then his heart, and finally his hand, he reached out across a lifetime. With a tender touch, more an embrace, his finger found the name, John's name, shining in moonlight that gave the brass a blue patina. He stared at the raised characters, and then through them, seeking to catch a glimpse of John on the other side. He closed his eyes and remembered a place nearby. The New Chatham train...

John, a strapping twenty-five year old, stood

before him, tall and slender, exuding the easy, wiry, physical presence of youth and the deep inner confidence of a man who knew who he was and where he was going. John had completed his training and was a proud member of the elite 5th Special Forces Group. He wore his Class-A uniform. Black spit-polished boots were bloused in the distinctive custom of the Airborne. His Green Beret proudly displayed the Special Forces insignia.

Clutching John's right arm tightly was Elizabeth Meyers, Lizzie, his girl friend since Junior High. Her sandy blond hair, tossed by a gentle breeze, fell across John's shoulder as she rested her head there. John squeezed Elizabeth's hand and kissed her softly on her forehead. It was a hard moment for them, but there were things George needed to say.

"So remember... Stay in the middle. Never volunteer for nothing...and don't let 'em get to know your name too easy," he told his son.

"Yes, Dad," John said laughing. *"That's the same thing you told me when I enlisted, and it's the second time you told me that this morning."* George smiled and nodded.

"A senior moment, huh?"

"Hey... you made it back from Vietnam okay.

I'll make it too. Six months in the Gulf, and I'll be home. Piece of cake." John looked down the platform toward the parking

lot. "I wish they would have come." George felt impotent, unable to change events. He glanced around nervously. A scattering of men in business suits stood waiting for the train. Another day at the office for them.

"They love you, son. You know that."

"Yeah."

"Your mother's scared to death. You're her baby, you know. First born. It's how women...how mothers get." George glanced at Lizzie. She smiled shyly. "Just look at you, son. You're a man, now." George smiled. "A warrior." John laughed, and slapped his father on the shoulder.

"Yeah. I know. Just like you were. Lean, mean, and almost bullet-proof."

A woman with a young boy at her side approached them. The child tugged at his mother's sleeve and pointed.

"Look mommy. A soldier!" The boy threw a child's salute at John, who smiled and returned the salute. The mother pulled her son away. George saw John glance away again at toward the parking lot,

hoping that his mother and sister might magically appear. But they didn't.

"Nothin's gonna' happen to me, dad. I'll..." The sudden wail of a train whistle turned their attention away. Up the tracks a bright headlight signaled the approaching train. The wooden platform trembled slightly beneath their feet. John pulled Elizabeth close to him. The moment George dreaded was here. The three of them stood frozen as the train pulled in, and with a final creak and bang, it stopped to gather the travelers. Sensing the moment, Elizabeth disengaged and George stepped forward to embrace his son. Around them, the other passengers hurriedly boarded the train. For them it was just a little trip into the city. They would return later that evening. For John it was the start of a journey into an unknown fraught with danger.

"I love you, Dad," John whispered as his father held him close, closer than he ever had in his life.

George tried to speak, but no words formed. His throat was dry. John pulled away gently and smiled. George nodded and placed his hand on his son's cheek, then stepped back to allow the few moments left to be between John and Elizabeth. Tears welled up in Elizabeth's eyes and spilled out. Her body trembled. Wisps of her hair matted on her wet cheeks.   John gently stroked the hair away and kissed her. He tasted her tears on the softness of her lips and inhaled the scent of her love. Embracing Elizabeth tightly, he kissed her neck and whispered, "I'll be back. Let's surprise every one at Christmas and get married." Elizabeth looked into his eyes.

"You really mean that?"   She felt lifted and thrilled.

"Yes."   His voice was hoarse.   He swallowed hard.

"Oh, John I love you.   I don't want you to go. I'm afraid and..."

"I'll be fine... And home for Christmas."   He kissed her quickly, hard on the mouth, then picked up his duffel bag and hefted it onto his shoulder. Smartly, he turned away and walked toward the train.   Once aboard he looked back and waved one last time.   Moments later, as the train disappeared down the track, George and Elizabeth were alone on the platform.

"God love you, son," George whispered as he placed his arm around Elizabeth. She got weak in the knees and sagged a bit. George held her close while she wept. She did not see or feel his tears as they melted into her golden locks.

The vision faded. George Boyajian was back at the monument, his finger still pressed against the name he loved, but his expression was now serene.

Behind George, three grungy clad, drunken teenagers sauntered into the park toward. They wore black engineer boots with dog chains strung around them, loose fitting blue jeans, and overly large, heavy plaid shirts. Two sported baseball caps cocked sideways. Their moonlit shadows moved along the deserted walkway, spilling onto George's as they stopped close by him. The leader of the motley group smeared his finger on the Vietnam War plaque.

"Hey man, where's Rambo? Like Rambo's gotta be here, man." He chuckled at the wittiness of his remark. The others laughed with him. A sudden hot rush of anger made George shake his head rapidly to clear away this rude intrusion into his privacy. He strained to ignore the young barbarians; to recapture the serenity of the emotional moment they had interrupted. A second teenager did an insulting mimic of 'Taps'.

"For God's sake," George said with precise pronunciation of each word, "This is a cathedral! Have respect!" The leader looked at George with a cynical smile. He glanced at his cohorts for support. "You got a problem, old dude?" He chuckled. "Yo, Man - We just looking for Rambo. With all these here dead mothers... Hey, gotta be Rambo too. Ain't that right, old dude?" Rising to his feet, George eyed the leader and then the others. He figured he could take down one big mouth before the others got him. If that was the price of protecting John's sanctity, he was ready to pay it.

"If you can't show respect, please leave."

"Yo, man... You're the one who needs to show respect," another boy said, opening his shirt and revealing the butt of a 9mm Glock automatic pistol.

"School the old dude, Frankie," said the leader.

"Yeah. Show him who we are, man," the third kid chimed in. They moved threateningly closer to George.

"Hey there old man," the leader said with a wide grin, "It's show time!" They closed in slowly, like a pack of hyenas on the Savannah, cornering what they thought to be an easy victim. George quickly glanced over his shoulder at John's name, as if to gather strength or perhaps to say good-bye. He saw the shadows of himself and his tormentors on the brass and granite. As he turned back to the confrontation the indistinct shadows of two strangers appeared from behind. A clear, deep voice cut through the tension.

"Is there a problem here?"

"Something we might help with?" the second stranger asked. George kept his eyes on the gang leader, now assuming that whatever the intruders tried to do the strangers behind him would help. The expression on the gang leader's face changed with the stranger's words. The young man's eyes grew wide and afraid, unable to comprehend. His bravado was gone as a great danger was suddenly staring him in the face. A cold blast of wind blew his arrogantly placed baseball cap off his head. It pushed him backward. He shuddered. His skin, a moment before flushed red with heated blood and arrogance yearning for action, had now turned a deathly gray.

"No. Uh... No man. No problem." George watched. The leader was responding to something the stranger had said, but George had heard no words.

"Yes sir," a different gang member said, hearing another voice that escaped George's detection. Respectfully, the frightened kid bowed his head.

"No problem, sir," the leader said again, his voice

now thin and fearful. "We uh...we didn't mean... What?" A flash of pain twisted his face in anguish, yet no one had touched him. "No, Man. We...we're sorry." The leader backed away. "Like really sorry, man..." He then turned and ran. The others quickly followed. George turned to thank the strangers. But they were gone. He looked all around the memorial park, then up and down the Town Square. But not a soul was in sight.

"I'll be damned," he muttered as he returned to John's plaque. "If that doesn't beat all." He then knelt again. "Listen Johnny... I'm gonna talk to them. Get them to come. To understand..." He felt a chill though no breeze had blown. "Oh God! Yes. I know you can see me, son." He touched John's name again, this time with the palm of his right hand. "You're here, aren't you...just on the other side. You know they didn't come to say good-bye at the station. But here...maybe... Maybe I can get them to understand. It's time. Maybe tomorrow."

CHAPTER TWO

VETERAN'S DAY

George stood in the warm kitchen with his back to his wife and daughter. The aroma of pancakes on the griddle blended mixed with brewing coffee and the tang of fresh squeezed oranges. His gaze was fixed on the rolling fields between the old farmhouse and the distant foothills. He was rehearsing his lines as though he were an actor in an impossible play, about to step on stage to face an unwelcoming audience. Yet he had no choice but to perform. After the events of last night at the monument George felt he was driven by a force he could not resist. He was a strong willed man but now something compelled him at act. He sipped from his gray ceramic coffee mug, then turned his gaze away from the outdoors, over his shoulder, to his daughter, his "baby", Jennifer. But Jenny was grown up. She was now in her late twenties; grown, married, divorced, and a single parent. A woman. Where had the years gone? She had George's brown hair, but not his blue eyes. Her's were duplicates of her mother's - brown, warm, bottomless pools that drew you into her soul. Jenny sat slumped at the oak, butcher-block kitchen table that George had built five years ago when they'd remodeled. Nicks, scars, and stubborn stains on the table bore witness to the kitchen being the center of life in their home; a locus of all good, bad, joyful, and tragic events which had befallen the Boyajian family. It all seemed to have centered around this sturdy, serviceable table in the kitchen. Jenny cradled her coffee mug between her delicate hands as if it were an offering to some omnipotent deity and she the supplicant seeking an answer to her prayer. She wore a loose fitting pale blue sweater, and jeans. Her pretty features bore the same troubled and distracted look George had observed for months. But they had become more pronounced over the course of the last few days. George's wife Carol, a stunning woman in her early sixties, sat next to Jenny.

George had fallen in love with Carol the first time he had seen her, and though heated passion had abated over the years, their was no diminishing of his deep and total love for her. Carol sat pensively with her left hand on Jenny's. She sensed George's his mood. Thirty-five years of marriage will do that. Her eyes narrowed. Her head tilted slightly to the right. George read the suspicion on her face;

she knew him too well, and all of his moods and methods.

"Listen, guys," he began, "I uh... Last night I had this experience. I can't explain it exactly, but it was, well, something." Jenny now looked at him too. Daughter and mother – a pair of skeptical bookends. "What I want... I mean what I'd like is for you two to come to town with me today... To..."

"Don't start, George," Carol curtly interrupted. "We settled all that long ago. Jenny's home to be with us. We're not going to that ceremony. And that's that!"

"But if you'll just..." he said stubbornly.

"For God's sake George!" Carol grasped Jenny's hand.

"Don't you think we have enough to deal with without your raking up more pain." George moved to the table and took their clasped hands in his.

"Jenny? Honey? Please. It's been so many years. Too many. It's time we..."

"No, George!" Carol said as she pulled her hand away. "It was yesterday! It will always be yesterday for us!" She extricated Jenny's hand from his and stood up.

"Please..." he begged. Carol shook hr head slightly and looked away. She was making an effort to control her emotions. She took a deep breath and looked at her husband.

"You're the one who let him go. He's a man, you said. He wants to serve his country, you said. You're the one who took him, in his uniform, to the American Legion Hall. You - the proud father! I don't need to see his name on that cold plaque. I buried my son next to your parents. His name is on the family stone. That's more than enough for me!"

"No dear... It's not about that."

"And what else is there but names?" she said sarcastically. "Lots of names. Others we knew and grew up with. Will seeing them bring them back to us? What is the point in going there again, and again, and again?" George knew that when Carol dug her heels in like this, nothing could move her. His only hope to get them to town was Jennifer.

"Please Jenny. Please trust me on this."

"Maybe I should go," Jennifer said bitterly. "After all, it may be my last chance before I'm in the ground next to Johnny."

"No! No!," George quickly said. "That's not what I meant, sweetheart."

"We have a living child here who needs us," Carol announced, wanting no more of this talk. "Jenny has to concentrate on only one thing - getting better."

"Well, damn it, I'm going. I haven't missed a year since..." George plucked his brown tweed sports coat from its peg on the nearby pine coat rack, thrusting his arms through the sleeves. He paused before the mirror on the top of the coat rack and adjusted his collar. He stared at the reflection of the Combat Infantryman's Badge in his lapel. He looked at Jennifer one more time, asking with his eyes for her to go with him. She turned her head away.

Carol's gaze stayed locked on him, showing neither anger or compassion.

George left, shutting the kitchen door gently behind him. He took a deep breath and exhaled. The pleasant scents of the farmhouse kitchen melted into a mist in the cold morning air. He inhaled again and was filled with the   scent of nearby pines. He walked toward his pickup, passing the door to his workshop in the barn. Down the path past the barn, the barren brown fields spread and stopped at the low, tree filled, rolling hills. He approached his old but reliable Chevy pickup. Heavy white clouds moved slowly across a brilliant blue sky with a swiftness that evoked something familiar and ingrained in his memory. These days his mental wanderings seemed to come with more and more clarity when emotionally intense events occurred in his life. George watched the clouds and drifting with them back in time.

A raw recruit in Vietnam - he and two fellow squad members take on nicknames and write them, with a black magic marker, on their helmet covers. George becomes "Tracker," one buddy becomes "Death Dealer," and the third becomes "Silent Death." As green as their fresh, dark, fatigues, they modeled themselves after the older guys; the nineteen and twenty year old enlisted combat veterans; and their twenty three year old captains. "Tracker" would come home. The other two, both with the word "death" in their nicknames, would not.

He reached the truck and the daydream ended. George climbed in, started the engine, and drove up the gentle slope to the country road that led to State Road 16, and town. He drove down the two lane black top, past his neighbors' farms - working family farms, a rare and fast disappearing enterprise. Stone walls, dating back to the American Revolution, lined both sides of the narrow road. He drove past the wide, single story, brown aluminum barn where the monthly farm animal auctions where held. The rusted and faded 'Help Wanted' sign swayed slowly in the wind. It seems the sign had beckoned forever, but George had never met anyone who had been hired there. Further down the road the John Deere dealership displayed the newest tractors, threshers, reapers, and trailers, all bright green with the distinctive yellow Deere logotype on their sides. Beyond the dealership, down a hill into a pocket valley, a spring fed pond where George used to catch stocked Rainbow Trout now hosted a flight of Canada Geese who had stopped to rest on their annual trip south. They paddled across the pond, darting their graceful necks below the surface to snap up what little nourishment remained before winter set in. George passed an abandoned farmhouse set back behind long dormant fields now occupied with shoulder high weeds. Its once white clapboards were stained with rusty, long, pale brown threads that seem to be tears shed by the abandoned structure. All of the windows were broken, no doubt shot out by local kids with B-B guns. George wondered about the fate of families who had once lived there. He imagined birthdays and Thanksgiving dinners. Were names of any of their kin engraved on the town's memorial? And what memories, sad or gay, might be contained, echoing within the walls of those now barren rooms? Did ghosts haunt the old house, peeking out when no one was looking? Did apparitions gather once again to celebrate birthdays and Thanksgivings? Or was the house merely an abandoned shell? In time boards would rot around rusted nails and the structure would collapse. Eventually there would be no physical sign that a family, that a history, had ever happened on that piece of earth.

These days George did not farm anymore. The local construction business, which had been a sometimes thing, had suddenly boomed since that fateful day of September 11, 2001. Growing numbers of people with money were moving upstate from New York City, seeking a rural haven should the unthinkable happen. The population had increased dramatically with scores of building permits still being filed every week at the county seat. George and the other tradesmen in the region were busy full time remodeling and rebuilding old estates, and doing finishing work on new ones. George's specialty was the accurate reproduction of eighteenth century American carpentry using many tools from that era. The word spread quickly that

George was a reliable, consummate craftsman. His talent was in great demand. Everyone wanted to make new things look old.

Nearing the town of New Chatham, he passed the Hess Oil distribution depot with its massive white storage tank. Then the Chevy dealership came into sight with its display of new pickups and SUV's out front. A quarter mile down the road, on his right, he passed the County Fair Grounds where once a year the toothless folks from the hill country, and the khaki clad week-enders from the big city, sporting fashionable logos on their T-shirts, mingled in odd ballet of country mouse - city mouse proportions. Beer drinkers were banished to a tent surrounded by police. Three hundred pound hungry fried-dough eaters, dressed in bib overalls and work boots, stood in long lines for tasty hot treats. Beyond the fair grounds, George could now see the brick smokestack of the ancient, long abandoned, shoe factory. At the start of the twentieth century, New Chatham had been a center of milling, leather tanning, and a bustling shoemaking industry. It had hosted a mixed population of nearly twenty thousand Italian, German, Polish and Scandinavian immigrants eager for jobs and a better life. But by mid-century, the mills, tannery and   factory had moved south and west. New Chatham settled back into its core industry, dairy. Now that too was passing into history. The real estate boom brought many of the locals work, but it would only last as long as there was land to build on or places to refurbish. It had a finite limit. Some people, like George Boyajian, had rediscovered many of the old-time crafts and trades. Others had become landscapers, contracting as the lawn mowers, gardeners, and ground's keepers of new estates fashioned from former farms. George knew that some of the locals resented the inconsiderate ways of the city people - taking two parking spaces, cutting ahead in lines, loud speaking, and disdainful of what they called 'provincial customs'.

"Call them what you will," he'd tell his friends, "there's more money and work floatin' around here than we've ever had before. So don't look a gift horse in the mouth or he might just bite you." And, to George, there was another benefit. Wilderness was returning to the region as the new, larger landholders, posted and patrolled their properties. To the chagrin of some of the locals, mostly seasoned poachers, the newcomers forbade hunting and fishing. But the result was a resurgence of wild turkeys, bear, and a rumored mountain lion or two. George liked that. He liked to hike in the woods behind his farm fields after a light rain, or early snow, and look for game tracks. He'd taken John hunting in those woods as a child, and had taught him how to hunt and shoot. But that now seemed like a hundred years ago.

George drove into town from the north. He passed the small playground with jungle gyms and slides; the new swimming pool; the old boot factory, now converted into loft apartments; and finally rows of clapboard houses that lined the road leading to the old iron bridge which spanned the diminutive Chatham River. Two thick, dark, stone columns, built in the late nineteenth century, stood at the entrance to the bridge - mute sentinels to the passage of time. He drove over the bridge. The roadway was pitted in a state of disrepair. He glanced downstream and marveled at the progress being made on the new bridge, a steel and granite structure, soon to be completed. Then this bridge would be removed, its iron sold as scrap, or so the town fathers promised. He slowly drove down Main Street. Cars were parked bumper to bumper filling all the available parking spots. Small shops faced each other on both sides of the street. An upscale gourmet market now stood where the old Grand Union had closed. Next to it was a mini-mall with a well stocked liquor store, a Coach outlet, an Old Navy store, and a Baskin-Robbins. On the other side of the street a bar, the New Chatham Public House stood, one of the few remnants of times past. Next door was a Chinese/Sushi restaurant, and on the other side a new, upscale, Martha Stewart furniture store. Beside the pub, there were only two of the original stores left on Main Street – Carmine's Barbershop, its red and white striped pole standing out front and spinning announcing there was still a refuge for men seeking merely a hair cut and not a hair styling experience; and Williamson's Hardware, with a green and white canvas awning that shaded its rippled, plate glass display window.

Ahead, George could see some familiar faces - townspeople gathering around the war memorial where he had been last night. Every year the same people gathered for the ceremony, though the ranks of the World War II and Korea veterans were noticeably thinning. George parked in the lot of the railroad station. As he always did, George peered down the platform where he and Elizabeth had said good-bye to John. Sometimes in his daydreams

George imagined that he could see John once more, but this time he stopped him from getting on that train. But then, no matter how hard he tried to manipulate the outcome, the dreams would end with John on the train, disappearing into the distant horizon.

George walked to the small War Memorial park. His blue and silver combat infantryman's badge, pinned on the lapel of his glen plaid sport jacket glinted in the bright sunlight. The five granite pillars, and their brass plaques, seemed less dramatic in the cold light of day. The New Chatham police had blocked off Main Street. Nearly one hundred townspeople were at the monument. Some of the older citizens, men and women, wore ribbons and military decorations on their chests. Younger onlookers stood in a silence, awed or curious about the ceremony. Many held small American flags. The town's American Legion honor guard stood at attention. The flag bearer was a middle-aged man with an ample paunch overhanging his wide, white, dress belt. His pale face was flushed red while a breeze made a wisp of his thinning hair dance on his forehead, the rest held down by his overseas cap. His flagstaff swayed, pulled by gusts. On either side of him stood honor guards with WW II vintage M1 rifles held at right-shoulder arms. They too, wore the same wide, white dress belts over their aging military uniforms. The men in the guard nodded toward George as he approached.

The American flag, on its pole, flapped in the wind, its ropes causing the same rattling sound George tuned into last night. From this point of view George could see the Thanksgiving displays in the stores. Soon they would be replaced by Christmas decorations, wreaths, lights, and bunting. George walked slowly and deliberately to a spot within a few yards of the memorial. He exchanged nods with a few more friendly faces and listened to the low hum of conversation as all waited for the ceremony to begin.

Mayor Andy Lockwood, dressed in a navy blue suit, white shirt, and a blue and red tie, was an imposing rotund man, with broad shoulders and a thick neck, shuffled papers in his hands and counted the number of voters assembling, identifying the loyal Republicans who always voted for him. He then noted the Democrats and Independents who rarely gave him their support. He made a mental reminder to talk to each one of them before they departed from the ceremony. With the influx of outsiders who might become voters, we knew he needed to expand his local base.

Mary Simpson, a short, weathered, red-haired woman in her early seventies, outfitted in bright green slacks, a red jacket and a white wool scarf walked up behind George.

"Morning, George," Mary said softly, startling him out of his reverie.

"Oh. It's you Mary. Not nice creeping up on a fellow that way." He smiled. "Good morning, Mare... How are you?"

"Just fine, George," she chuckled, "for an old creepy battle-ax, that is. How's Carol?"

"Fine, thanks." Mary glanced around furtively.

"And Jenny?" she asked, her voice lowered.

"She's okay."

"But how is she doing, George?" Mary asked softly.

"She's doing just fine, Mare. She's staying with us for a while. We took her up to Albany...to the Medical Center. They've got a good program up there. Did a needle biopsy. We're waiting for the results."

"Carol mentioned it. They do such wonders today, now don't they?"

"Yes... I guess they do." George's jaw clenched. Mary took his hand.

"You know, I remember when you had Jennifer. All those years after Johnny. Why Carol had given up all hope of conceiving again, and those doctors told her to forget it. Hah! And then, out of the blue, there was Jenny! 'Our beautiful little miracle,' you called her." Mary leaned closer. Her voice was hushed. Private. "This illness, if it is... you know... Well, there's just so much they can do now. So much more hope. And new things every day."

"You're right. And thanks, Mary." He genuinely meant it.

"If there's anything I can do... Anything... You just ask. You hear me, George Boyajian?"

"I do, Mary. I surely do." She reached up and kissed him on the cheek. "This town might be getting big, but the folks who count love you, and your family. We'll never get so big that we don't take care of our own. You hear?"

"I know." George glanced toward John's name on the nearby plaque. "You know, Mare, I was talking to Johnny last night." Mary nodded and smiled.

"What did he say, George?"

"He said," George whispered in a conspiratorial tone, "that he thinks we ought to have Christmas this year."

"Oh George! That's wonderful. Whatever I can do, let me know. I bake today. Maybe I'll bring you over something sweet for the holidays." She then handed him a single red rose. "Seems this has become a ritual. Now you take care." George watched her walk away. Mary Simpson, like so many friends in New Chatham, was an extension of his family. He sniffed the fragrant flower. The sun glinted off the brass tablets, as though the names inscribed there were shouting for attention. The bronze letters seemed like so many tiny doors that were open to allow the light from the other side to shine through. He felt a hand on his shoulder.

"George," said Tom Jennings, extending his hand and shaking George's vigorously. Tom was nearly six feet six inches tall and slender as an old illustration of Ichobod Crane. His face was just as angular. Jenning's gray postal service uniform was starched and pleated in a military fashion. "Carol and Jenny not here?"

"They just can't do it, Tom. I tried, Lord knows, but it's still too much for them. Maybe next year..."

"Sure. See you later." As Tom walked away Larry Williamson, confined to a wheelchair, rolled into view. Larry wore a jungle fatigue hat and a fatigue jacket with staff sergeant's stripes on the sleeves and his combat infantryman's badge pinned to his chest. He had served in Vietnam with George where his encounter with a Soviet-made anti-personnel mine had left him a paraplegic.

"Larry," said George stepping toward the hardware store proprietor. He patted his old friend on the shoulders.

"Alone?" Larry asked. As George nodded, Larry looked over at the plaque bearing John Boyajian's name.

"You know I..." Larry was interrupted by the New Chatham High School Band as they struck up *God Bless America*. Silently, George stood at attention, his arms to his sides, his legs together. The music, and the sharp crisp red and white stripes and silver stars on a field or deep blue that fluttered above them once again brought to the fore the realization of how their lives had forever been changed by their war, and for George, John's war as well. Two soldiers, one standing, one irreparably crippled, experienced a common, silent, personal memory. The band finished and Mayor Lockwood stepped out in front of the silent granite pillars.

"Residents of New Chatham and visitors, we welcome you to this observance of Veterans Day - a day of homage and respect for all who have served..." he droned on in politician talk until he turned toward the five plaques behind him. "The names of our families, friends and neighbors here enshrined - generations of our town's young men, and women, defending America, bearing witness to the terrible price freedom demands. We honor the men and women whose names are forever inscribed on these plaques, and their families who have endured such a great loss, and those who today serve and wait." The Mayor stepped forward and placed a wreath at the base of the W.W.I pillar. Lonnie Sanderson, a W.W.II veteran, with help from a friend supporting him, bowed, and placed a flowered wreath under the plaque bearing the names of the W.W.II dead. Marjorie Blackman, the widow of Terry Blackman, who was killed in 1952 at the Yalu River, when the Chinese Communist Army entered that war, followed with a wreath under the name of her husband, and his lost comrades. Then, Larry Williamson wheeled forward and placed a bouquet of flowers under the Vietnam plaque. Finally, George Boyajian stepped forward with the single rose that Mary Simpson had given him for the Gulf War plaque. He touched the only name - John Boyajian. George said a silent prayer, saluted, and stepped back among his comrades - a tight circle of honor and an unspoken bond among the combat veterans present.

"Let us all take a moment of silence," the Mayor continued, "to honor all of our veterans among us and especially these whose names are here...engraved in brass on stone, and forever in our hearts." The tinny sounds of the lanyard tapping against the hollow aluminum pole, and the large American flag, snapping in the breeze above, traveled through the town center. For a long moment, the townspeople present bowed and prayed silently as one. Then Judy Carmichael, a pretty sixteen year old with a zest for life and world conquering dreams, the lead trumpet player in the High School band, stepped forward. She lifted her shiny, silver, trumpet to her lips and played a mournful and heartfelt Taps. George and Larry shivered at that simple melody they had heard so many times before.

"Ladies, and gentlemen, that concludes this year's remembrance of our veterans," Mayor Lockwood announced. "Thank you for attending." He moved off to have words with the voters as the crowd broke up by twos and threes. People strolled back to their cars, or to the nearby stores that were open for Veteran's Day sales.

"Hey, George!" The Mayor called out. George and Larry who were leaving the park, turned to him. "Wait up George." George and Larry waited as Lockwood joined them. "George, I want to do right by you, and by John."

"What is it, Andy?" George asked.

"We uh... the thing of it is... well, we might need more room." George could see Lockwood was uncomfortable.

"Room?" George asked.

"We've got people from town, and the county, in the 554th MP Reserve Unit. They're called up – heading for Iraq. And there's the two Henson boys with the 10th Mountain Division plus Lonnie Fredericks' son with the Rangers. They're in Afghanistan..."

"So you might have to add another plaque."

"Christ, I hope not, but the town council wants to be prepared. I mean we're not expecting anything but..."

"Yeah... but," George said, looking back at John's plaque. Andy Lockwood put his arm on George's shoulder.

"At first we thought, if it came to it, we'd put one plaque for Afghanistan and one for Iraq. But then we decided on one plaque. I mean they're sending our kids all over the world now...this terrorism business. Preemptive."

"It's all blending into one," George muttered.

"The world's cops," Larry added. "Our kids...For what?" Andy Lockwood was a staunch Republican, but as Tip O'Neil, the once Speaker of the House of Representatives used to say, 'All politics are local...' Lockwood avoided confrontation with his hometown people whenever possible.

"We thought we'd add plaques, if we have to, in the space under John's...if that's all right with you."

"You don't have to ask me, Andy," George said. "I don't own the space on that monument."

"No," Lockwood quickly replied, "but John does, which is why we want your blessing."

"Do what you need to do Andy. God help us all if we start adding more names to that monument."

"I pray we don't. How's Carol and Jenny?"

"Fine. Just fine." The Mayor hustled off to press some flesh. George glanced over at John's plaque one more time. It looked lonely. "I guess if it has to be, John could use some company." Larry nodded and wheeled his chair toward Main Street. "Just a sec, Lar," George told his friend. He trotted over to Mayor Lockwood, chatted with him for a minute, and then returned.

"What was that all about?" George stared into Larry's eyes, one brother in arms to another.

"I told him...well sort of volunteered that if... or when..." He looked away from Larry for a moment, past Main Street, far, as if he could see the forbidding mountains of Afghanistan and the endless desert sands between the Tigris and Euphrates Rivers, "... the news comes to another family in town to call me. Maybe I can...you know..."

"Maybe we both can, pal."

An hour later George drove down the gravel driveway to the one story ranch house that was the local veteran's organization headquarters. Small pebbles bounced up against the undercarriage of the truck like hail. Off to the right was a field occupied by rows of picnic tables and brick barbecue pits. To his left, the ground sloped down to a pond stocked with fat rainbow trout where the vet's group held its annual fishing derby for the kids. An oversized stuffed figure of Santa Claus was propped up against the headquarters' flag pole. Next to it was a hand painted sign that read "Annual Xmas Toy Drive."

A long dining room where they held ceremonial dinners and events occupied the front half of the building, while the back half was fitted out with a bar that ran the length of the back wall. Behind it was a large picture window that overlooked the pond.

"How the hell are you!" shouted Robbie Crippens, red faced and portly, as he mopped the bar with a rag. "Get you a cold one?"

"Too early for me, Robbie. How about a Pepsi?"

"You got it." Robbie reached behind into a cooler and extracted a frosty can, popped it open and handed it to George along with a tall, ice filled glass. "Red, white and blue can. The right drink for today."

"Thanks." George poured the dark liquid and lifted it to no one in particular. "To absent friends."

"Here, here..." A half of a dozen veterans at the far end of the responded. George knew them all. Another group of older men were wrapping toys in gaily colored paper. He smiled at the contrast - the veterans taking time and what little spare money they have to help the less fortunate, and the professional veterans; the would-be and wannabe heroes whose lives were changed forever by war. 'Well,' George thought, 'It doesn't matter they all paid the price of admission...'

"Hey George," Seth Williams said as he approached. Seth was average height and sported a paunch. He limped. He and George had been bounced around together in Vietnam, and the punishment on Seth's body now claimed his senior years - arthritic knees and cervical and lumbar discs compressed to where any activity was painful. Seth joined him. They shook hands.

"Ain't seen you in a while, George."

"I've been real busy." Seth eased onto a stool.

"Hey Robbie, let me have a coffee, will you?" Robbie nodded. "That time of year, again, George."

"Yeah. They come faster now, don't they?"

"And they don't get easier...I mean your Johnny."

"No. Never will." Seth accepted a coffee mug from Robbie. "Thanks, Robbie." He took a long sip while staring through the glass window at the pond beyond.

"Sometimes it seems just like yesterday, huh? "Or like maybe it's all going to happen again tomorrow. I guess we had some times, George."

"I'll drink to that." They clinked drinks. "And to the strange ones like those Psyops Spooks?" George said.

"Yeah, I remember them. Two Harvard Phds with the military intelligence insignia. No rank."

"And that interpreter of theirs," George added. "The spooky lookin' dude with one eye that sort of snaggled off into space."

"That was a real plan to end the war, huh?"

"Damn near ended us," George mused.

The down wash from the Huey's rotor pummeled their chests causing their jungle fatigues to flap wild as if in a storm. Vibrations caused the thin skinned bird to shudder in syncopation with pounding hearts. His legs, dangling over the edge of the Huey were washed in sunlight, his upper torso hidden in shadow. The wind flattened the dry ginger ale brown rice stalks below. Shoveling himself off the Huey, George fell to the ground with his knees bent in a modified parachute landing fall. A twisted ankle in this clearing would make him a slow moving target. He wouldn't hear the report of an AK-47, but anticipated the sledge hammer blow to shoulder, or the splinter of the bones of his skull above the bridge of his nose. From the corner of his eye he saw Seth sprinting toward the dark wall of jungle a hundred yards away. George inhaled deep gulps of one hundred and twenty degree air; his lungs burning as if he were running the Wannamaker Mile. The straps of his eighty pound pack cut into his shoulders as he counted the strides between him and the tree line glancing rapidly from right to left and back to his front to see if anyone fell. With two yards to go he leapt, passing from the brilliant yellow sunlight of the abandoned, dried up rice paddy to the cooler jungle darkness. Slumping in a heap, George curled up behind a tree, his rifle thrust forward. Hot, salty sweat burned his eyes, soaked his clothes, and attracted flying and crawling insects – an incredible variety. The company of South Vietnamese irregulars he and Seth were with organized itself and took off toward the mountains to the east. A few men in front of George, Daiuy Van, Captain Van, led the way. George was comfortable with Daiuy Van. He'd been fighting this war for twenty years; back to fighting the Viet Minh. It was amusing that the U.S. Army made George advisor to Daiuy Van. There wasn't anything about infantry small unit tactics that George could teach the Daiuy. What George and Seth did bring, however, was the power of their radio that could summon rotary winged carriers of rockets and miniguns. They could cause the sky to rattle as one hundred and five millimeter projos rent the air and tore into the jungle. They could cause speeding silver shapes to appear in the sky, and ugly yellow clouds burning black to fill the jungle with gagging fumes and burning corpses. They could summon slow moving olive drab birds piloted by the bravest men in the war, with large red crosses painted across white backgrounds.

It was dusk as George and Seth sat with Daiuy Van.

"Ba xi de," said Daiuy Van nodding to George, and then to the dark hills surrounding the small valley. "Many Vee Cee tonight." George accepted the old warrior's canteen and took a sip of the pungent, fish juice and kerosene tasting liquid. In the gathering darkness The first Harvard Ph.d, late of the U.S. Army Military Intelligence School, Fort Devens, Massachusetts, tapped George on the shoulder. He spun, plucking his .45 from its holster, thumbed back the hammer and thrust the weapon squarely into the abdomen of the terrified psychological warrior. The man turned a ghostly white. George lowered the pistol.

"Don't come up behind us. Got it?"

"Got it, sergeant," said the spook regaining his breath. "How deep should my foxhole be?"

"Well," said Seth, "that is a matter of discretion. Personally, I like to get mine down to the water table."

"Okay. What I needed to know." The young

doctor trotted off to inform his compatriot.

"Down to the water table?" George, Daiuy Van, and Seth had a good laugh.

While Daiuy Van's company, the Mot Mot Ba, the "One One Three," formed a three hundred and sixty degree perimeter, the sound of an entrenching tool chopping into the jungle soil hovered over the gathering. The spooks were digging.

Later they set up a loudspeaker and had their interpreter rapid fire a string of Vietnamese words echoing up the walls of the valley. George listened carefully; making out a few words he could understand. "Surrender. Hectare. Rice."

Good luck, thought George, hunkering down. IUt didn't take long for all hell to break loose as a shower of rocket propelled grenades answered the psyops announcement. A cry of pain called out nearby but none of the rockets reached them. George and Seth crawled over and felt the earth give way to a void before him, - the cavernous yap of the foxhole. Low groans of pain came from the bottom. Plucking the red filtered flashlight from his web gear, George turned it on. Before him, six feet below the surface of the ground lay the second Ph.D. spook. Across the foxhole was what was left of the man's hammock where he had strung it several feet below the surface.

In the dim red light, George could see the unnatural angle of the man's leg and knew with a certainty that it was broken.

"Probably get a medal for that stunt," Seth said. No attack came that night, though George, Seth, and Daiuy Van remained alert until sunrise. George figured that the stupidity of the effort was what probably had saved their lives – any unit dumb enough to expect a loudspeaker to get the NVA to surrender probably wasn't worth the ammunition to destroy. They never did see the Psysops guys again, and were left alone in their little corner of the war.

"To Phds," said Seth raising his coffee cup. "Sure knew how to screw up a war."

"Yeah," said George, "and to the horses they rode in on." The television over the bar was showing an Iraqi road. Plumes of black smoke came from a Hum-Vee.

"Turn that thing off," said Seth angrily. "That's 101st for God's sake. Our old unit - out there like sitting ducks. Damned politicians ought to be there instead." George patted Seth on his shoulder.

"I got to get going, pal."

"Happy Thanksgiving, George."

"Yeah...you too."

CHAPTER THREE

THANKSGIVING - PAST AND PRESENT

Later that month, on Thanksgiving night, George and Carol were alone. A wide planked pine table dominated the center of their small dining room, embraced by eight tall, cane-backed chairs. An antique green hutch, displaying a nearly full set of Manchester-Bavaria China, stood against one walnut paneled wall. On the opposite wall, above an oak sideboard, an oil painting of a cheery old spinster, done in the late eighteenth century by a forgotten Boston artist, smiled down on the diners.

"The chicken is really good," George said.

"It's glazed with honey and ginger," Carol answered, not looking at him.

"Delicious." They sat in silence and nibbled at their roast chicken dinner, garnished with candied yams, walnut stuffing, and homemade cranberry sauce. There was a mild tension in the air, but only small talk.

Later, Carol cleared the dishes and went into the

kitchen to fetch coffee for George, and a cinnamon-apple pie. She knew that George had something on his mind that he was having difficulty discussing. It made her uneasy. He always paid her a compliment, usually about her cooking, before he brought up a controversial or important subject.

The kitchen TV was on CNN. There were six more Marines killed in Iraq by what they now called "insurgents". That was interrupted by breaking news had been another terrorist attack in Jerusalem, killing nine school children on a bus. The Israelis had responded immediately with rockets, fired from two helicopter gunships, at four suspected Hezbollah and Hamas bomb factories. She stared at the violent images of injured and dead Israeli kids, and exploding rockets. Those scenes slowly dissolved back in time for Carol.

It was October, 1990. George, Jennifer, and she were eating dinner in the kitchen and watching the evening news. The CNN correspondent stood on the docks in Saudi Arabia as American tanks were driven off transport vessels. Those images became Black Hawk helicopters taking off over tent cities bustling with American soldiers.

"We haven't gotten a letter from John since he's been there," Carol had remarked softly.

"Honey, you know John can't write us now," George answered. *"His missions are black ops."*

"Black ops?" said Jennifer. *"My God, daddy. You sound like a Tom Clancy novel."*

"What John is doing is no novel, sweetheart. I'll bet you five ways from Sunday he's deep inside Iraqi territory right now." Carol saw herself put down her fork and knife and rise silently, leaving the room with her hands pressed to her face.

"Mary Simpson brought this by yesterday," she said softly, as she entered the dining room with the cinnamon-apple pie. "She's so sweet. A real friend." She poured a cup of strong black coffee for George. "Do you want some ice cream with it?"

"No. This is fine. Sit down. I want to talk." Carol frowned, then settled into her chair and sipped her cup of tea.

"Is this about Jennifer?" Her somber look tugged at his heart. George took a deep breath.

"About Jennifer, and us." Carol kept her emotions under control.

"Oh?" she said flatly.

"I really miss not having Jennifer and David here

tonight, for Thanksgiving."

"She wanted to be here, but it's Harold's turn to have David and she wanted to be with him too." What Carol left unsaid was that their daughter was afraid this might well be her last Thanksgiving with her young son David. The needle biopsy had been, as many are, inconclusive. They take only a few cells – a hit or miss proposition. The next procedure was to do a lumpectomy. George read Carol's thoughts. He fought his emotions by clearing his throat. He then slid his hand over to Carol's, pausing as his fingers touched her wedding ring.

"Sweetheart, what say we have ourselves a real Christmas this year?" She abruptly pulled her hand away.

"Where does this come from, George? Maybe you forgot?" she said sarcastically. "It's the day they came here to tell us Johnny was dead! That's Christmas to us. Good God, George. All these years you've been the one saying we have to respect...to remember."

"Yes. I did. But it's time to stop."

"Oh it is? Why? Because you say so?" Her anger was rising. "Well, I say no! I say let sleeping dogs lie!"

"I believe... Look Carol, what we're doing is

wrong. We can't...we shouldn't live in the past anymore." She glared angrily at her husband, even as tears formed in her eyes.

"It was yesterday for me. Do you hear? It will always be yesterday for me!" But George couldn't let it go.

"There isn't a day that passes that I don't think of John," he said plaintively. When I'm on a job, I remember... just a boy, coming with me. When I work around here, sometimes I look up, expecting to see him bringing me a cup of coffee or running to tell me the latest joke from school. No. I haven't forgotten." George slowly took Carol's hand again. "If anything, love, I remember him better and clearer than before. And if you had been at the memorial that night with me..." Carol raised her hand.

"Don't start that mystical junk again. You and your memorial...and your shadows. You think they put it up for John?" She snickered. "They put it up for themselves. For their guilt!"

"It's not about guilt. It's about healing. But we've...I..." George poked his chest with his index finger, "I admit it. I've turned Christmas into some kind of wake, and it's wrong. It's very wrong. For us, and Jennifer. And for David."

"Oh really?" Carol responded sharply. "You

remember John's last Christmas home? You had him wear his uniform to Church on Christmas Eve. You sat there all puffed up with pride."

"What was I supposed to do? He wanted to serve his country. That was his choice. His life."

"Well, it certainly was, wasn't it!" she shouted, slamming her fist on the table. George winced as if a knife had been plunged into his flesh.

"Just think about it," George said softly. "Please. Jennifer will be here for the lumpectomy the week before Christmas. And David's coming a few days later. Maybe we could do it for them... For healing...?"

"The only healing that interests me is Jennifer's," Carol told him. Her tone of voice had finality to it. "Can you get that through that stubborn, thick, Armenian, head of yours?" She went back to sipping her tea, her hands trembling. She no longer looked at him. As angry and hurt as she was, George knew his wife. The seed had been planted. He held out hope that she would think about it, and perhaps reconsider. He could only wait and see.

At that same time, in her apartment on the Upper East Side of Manhattan, Jennifer pushed the turkey dressing on her plate in methodical circles with her fork. She averted her eyes from Harold. Their divorce had been unnecessarily painful, with both of them soothing their own pain by inflicting more on the other partner. David, a headstrong seven year old, with a growing sense of independence and self-reliance, ate quietly. He glanced from Jennifer to Harold, and waited. He had learned that since the divorce, silence between them was a good thing.

"Place looks nice," said Harold looking around the two bedroom apartment. Its mauve walls and white trimmed molding seemed to frame the emptiness of their lives. The slight echo of their voices, caused by a lack of furnishings and carpeting, accentuated the effect.

"Thank you," Jennifer answered, coolly.

"Great meal too." Harold, who was five foot nine, wore his hair long. He had gold rimmed glasses that sat well on his round face. He dressed in expensive designer clothes. It seemed to Jennifer, as their marriage went downhill, that he was miscast in life as a media salesman. The appearance he gave was that of a defense lawyer, or surgeon, or hit-shot agent with a wife at home and a younger mistress on the side. Harold reached out for Jennifer's hand. Reflexively, she pulled away from him.

"Don't," she whispered.

"I'm just trying to..."

"David honey, are you finished?" she said, cutting Harold off.

"Yes mommy."

"Why don't you go play in your room?"

"Okay." David rose from his chair, the wooden legs screeching against the bare parquet floor, and left the dining area. He looked back at his father with misgiving - the glare of the only true male in his mother's life.

"That wasn't necessary," said Harold reaching for the dark green bottle of Yellow Tail Cabernet. He refilled his glass first, and then poured some for Jennifer.

"I think it was," she said with fatigue. "He's been through enough without having to witness whatever the hell it is you think you're doing."

"I'm concerned. I care." Jennifer laughed.

"That's why we divorced? Because you care? Look, I don't want to get into it. It's over. We did the Thanksgiving thing for David. We can both be proud of ourselves. No blood spilled in front of our son." Jennifer rose, lifted a few plates from the table, and took them to the kitchen.

"Here, I'll help you." Harold took more plates and followed her. In the kitchen, Jennifer held the wineglass in her left hand and leaned back against the white enamel sink. A twisted smile appeared on her face.

"What?"

"You."

"What do you mean?"

"Caring. Helping. I just find it all amusing."

"That's the wine talking."

"No, it's not enough wine talking." Jennifer left the kitchen and went back to the table to refill her glass. He followed her.

"Don't you think you've had enough?"

"You colossal ass. What difference does it make now?"

"You don't know... You've got to take care."

"The doctor seemed pretty damn positive. What do I have to look forward to? Getting cut open and then placed in the family plot next to my brother?"

"It's unfair...what's happening to you. But he was another story." Jennifer scowled.

"And what the hell is that supposed to mean?" Harold got up and went back to the kitchen. He began scraping the plates into the trash bin.

"C'mon," said Jennifer, sauntering after him. "Just what the hell do you mean by that remark?"

"He got what killers of civilians deserve."

"You ass. He served his country. He did his duty."

"Like a fool. I wouldn't."

"No you selfish bastard, you wouldn't."

"And look who's dead." Jennifer lunged at Harold and slapped the back of his head. The blow caught Harold off guard. He reeled across the kitchen floor and fell against the wall, barely keeping his balance. Instinctively, he stepped back toward Jennifer with his right fist clenched. At that moment David raced into the kitchen, tears streaming from his eyes, and flailed away at Harold's legs with his fists.

"Uncle John was a hero! He was a hero! I hate you! I hate you!" Jennifer knelt and took David in her arms. The boy cried on her shoulder.

"Go Harold. Just go!" She stroked the back of David's head. "You're absolutely right, honey. Uncle John was a hero. A great hero." They hugged one another as they listened to Harold get his coat and slam the door behind him. There was a long moment of silence. Then David pulled away from his mother's shoulder and looked into her eyes.

"Mommy? What's going to happen to me if you die?"

"Oh...no darling," said Jennifer squeezing David tightly. "I'm not going to die."

"But what if you do?

"Then," said Jennifer taking a deep breath, and looking directly into David's eyes, "you'll go to live with Grandma and Grandpa."

"And you'll be in heaven with Uncle John?"

"Yes, Dear."

Harold stepped out into the brisk night air. Hands in his pockets, an English Oval cigarette in his mouth, he strolled aimlessly over to Fifth Avenue. He studied the elaborate, animated, Christmas displays in the store windows - cheery elves, a mellow, rotund Santa, whimsical toy trains, pink and blue sparkling reindeer - all competing for the attention of shoppers. Happy families, pumped up by that morning's Macy Thanksgiving Day parade, toted shopping bags filled with gaily-wrapped presents as they passed by him in both directions. He heard children's laughter and thought about David's recrimination – 'I hate you... I hate you!' Self-pity welled up within until there was no room for any other emotion. Harold sobbed. The laughing Santa on the other side of a nearby store window seemed to mock and chide him.

"Jesus," muttered Harold. "I'm a mess." He took a deep breath, lit another cigarette, and moved down Fifth Avenue, despising every happy family he saw along the way, and dreading returning to his empty apartment. The lit sign of an upscale bar, off Fifth on Forty-Fourth Street, beckoned. Yes, we're open on a holiday, it announced. Green Gothic letters, "Callahan's", were etched into thick plate glass. They curtained his view of the inside.

A long, dark bar, backed by ceiling high mirrors, held shelf upon shelf of bottled relief. The sight of it eased his pain. A few patrons sat on bar stools, chatting and sipping. The lone bartender, an average size man with dark hair, bright eyes, and pleasant features, drew a long draft. He wore black trousers, a white shirt, and a green and red holiday tie. The bar felt comfortable enough. It seemed a safe port from the storm engulfing him - life, death, love, marriage, family, war, peace. They were all now confusing concepts, with little relevance to his seemingly aimless and empty life. A fleeting thought... Harold wondered if he had what it took to climb the stairs to the roof and jump. He knew, as Jennifer had pointed out as their marriage self-destructed, he was indeed a coward. Her brother John, wasn't. He was. John was dead. He was alive. David loved John. He hated his father. It's easy to hate a coward when larger than life fools go off to war, proclaiming they are fearless. Dead, you can never confront their bravado.

Harold pulled back a barstool with a loud, scraping sound. The bartender approached. Harold took out his cigarette pack and flipped one into his mouth. Then he noticed there were no ashtrays on the bar.

"No smoking the big apple bars," the bartender said. He nodded and put his smokes away.

"Right. I've got to quit, anyway. Johnny Walker Black. Rocks."

"You got it." The bartender quickly returned with a square edged glass of amber liquid and ice. He placed it neatly in front of Harold, on a napkin with the bar's name printed in green letters on it.

"Run a tab for you, Sir?"

"Yeah, sure. Why not?"

Three scotches later the bartender settled in front of Harold.

"No Thanksgiving dinner tonight?"

"Yeah. They threw me out. I got no place to go."

"Whoa. It can't be that bad." The bartender

stepped back and gave Harold a friendly smile. "You dress like you got money... No ring on your finger, so it can't be marriage problems."

"Bar room psychiatrist, huh?"

"Nope. Just a damned good bartender." He extended his arms wide. "There ain't much I haven't done, or seen, or hasn't been talked about in here. Name's Danny Callahan." He extended his hand to shake.

"Harold Michaels." They shook hands.

"You say Harry or Harold."

"It doesn't matter."

"It don't matter." Callahan smiled. "Those are words that bring it all back."

"What?"

"That's what we used to say - 'It don't matter.' You know, like if you said it, things didn't really matter except waking up, surviving, and getting back to the world."

"The army, huh?" Why do some guys never talk about it, and others work it into every conversation? Harold thought to himself. His ex-father-in-law, George, was one of the silent ones. He looked at Callahan and thought of George warmly. He liked Jenny's dad.

"Yeah. Vietnam. Can't you tell by the gray hair?"

Callahan laughed. "I never thought I'd get this old. Middle age. Who the hell would've believed it?"

Harold

sipped his drink. The scotch had now joined the wine, and he was mellowed out.

"You see much action?"   Callahan's smile vanished and his eyes grew cold. "Not with my body."

"I don't follow you."

"I was drafted in sixty-six. Went through Basic and Advanced Infantry Training. Then Jump School. For the money and the bloused boots. You know, come home on leave to the neighborhood. West side. Hell's Kitchen. Strutting around with my jump wings and glider patch. The girls loved it. But I broke my back on my second jump."

"They discharge you?"

"Hell no. They healed me. In those days they were so hard up they were taking guys with fused spines and nine toes. They fixed me up and sent me down to Texas - Fort Sam Houston. Trained me as a medic. I did my first tour at the 45th Evac in Long Binh in early sixty-eight, and my second in seventy."

"Let me buy you a drink, Danny." Callahan looked around. There were only two customers left in the bar.

"Sure. He filled a shot glass with peppermint schnapps. "Happy holidays," he toasted, and knocked it down in one gulp. "Thanks." Danny poured Harold another drink, then leaned back against the bar. "There I am - you know that's how all war stories start, 'there I was, surrounded by an NVA regiment...' Then, you say, 'no shit.'" He chuckled. "Anyway, here I am at the 45th, and one day the Medevac chopper lands on the pad outside the ER. They roll this grunt in on a gurney, and..." Danny paused, the levity gone. He swallowed hard. "...and here's this guy from Fort Benning that I knew. Then another one and another - all of the guys I trained with were in a unit that was hit that day."

"That's some coincidence." It made Harold uneasy to hear Callahan's story, but he wasn't' sure why.

"See, I should have been with those guys out in the bush, and instead I'm back in the rear."

"It wasn't your choice."

"It don't matter. They were busted up and I was alive in the rear." Callahan became silent, staring off at something Harold couldn't understand.

"Was it tough on you? I mean when you got back?"

"I don't remember much of sixties or seventies. I finally woke up in the eighties."

"Let me buy you another drink." Danny poured another shot of schnapps.

"I felt sorry for myself for a long, long, time. I'll tell you Harold, that's a song nobody else in the world needs to hear more than once."

"What did you do?"

"Bounced around. Traveled. Lots of meaningless jobs. I burned up a lot of life being sorry for me."

"Yeah," said Harold. "I know how that can be."

"So you know. All of us dream about what might be. But, it's the ones who make it happen, and I don't mean being no Tiger Woods. Not like that. You wake up in the morning and you're glad you got one more day. Or you can say to yourself - oh Christ, another day in front of me. That's your play."

"How did you have the uh..."

"Guts?"

"Yeah. The guts to make that call." As if on cue, the door to the bar opened. Callahan looked past Harold and his whole demeanor changed. His face brightened. Harold turned to see a strikingly beautiful middle-aged woman entering. Her blond hair was pulled back through a Yankees baseball cap.

Faint lines on her face revealed her maturity. Harold knew Callahan didn't see the lines. Her beauty was ageless. Under a Navy P-coat, she wore a pastel green sweatshirt. Tight Levi's fell over tooled Dan Post boots. Reaching the bar, she leaned forward and kissed Callahan lightly on the cheek.

"Kathy, meet a pal of mine. This is Harold."

"Hi there Harold," she said extending her hand.

"A pleasure."

"I missed you... So thought I'd come by to tell you that," she said to Danny. "That's all." They kissed and she left. Harold watched her exit the bar.

"That's it? She missed you and came by to give you a kiss?" Danny smiled.

"You asked where'd I get the guts? There it goes. When I ran into Kathy I was a pretty sorry son of a bitch. I don't know what she saw in me, but she listened. She listened until I got tired of telling the same stories. One morning I woke up, looked at her next to me, and knew I was one lucky hombre. She was a gift that gave me the rest of my life."

"You're a lucky guy, Danny Callahan."

iHiHH

"You got that right. We may come in this life alone, and go out alone. But nobody makes it through this life alone."

"Yeah." Harold looked down into his drink. There

was a long awkward pause. Callahan put his hand on Harold's shoulder.

"I suggest you go do the right thing, Harold. Whatever's eatin' at you - wife, girl friend, money... whatever." He smiled. "But I imagine you already know the right thing to do."

CHAPTER FOUR

A WAITING GAME

It was the Monday before Christmas Eve. The Albany Medical Center staff was already winding down in anticipation of the holiday beginning on Friday. Emergencies couldn't be helped, but elective surgery was non-existent at this time of year. Jennifer's lumpectomy was not exactly elective, but it might have waited until after the holidays, or at least that's what some of the operating room staff chatted about. In any case, it was eleven o'clock, and she was in recovery. She would stay overnight, and then spend the week, and Christmas, in New Chatham. Dr. Alicia Ortiz, her oncologist, had told Carol and George that the pathology wouldn't be back for a week because of the holiday.

Jennifer was still in twilight-land as Carol and George stood next to her bed in the recovery room. The only other patient there was a six-year-old who had her tonsils out. She was clutching her worried parents' hands and moaning. The sight and sound upset Carol. George stroked Jennifer's hair. He leaned down and kissed her forehead. She stirred and breathed deeply, but didn't awaken.

"She looks so pale," Carol said.

"It's the anesthesia. She'll be fine. She's a strong girl," George said with assurance.

"Is she? I wonder." It was not like Carol to be pessimistic. Did she know something, George wondered? Jennifer's doctor, Alicia Ortiz, walked into the recovery room. She had changed from her operating room blues to her white hospital coat. She greeted the Boyajians and looked at Jennifer's chart. She then looked up at the vitals monitor above the bed.

"She's just fine," Dr. Ortiz said. "Good pulse. Normal temp. No problems." She leaned closer to Jennifer. "Jenny?" she said. "Hey there sleepyhead. Your folks are here." Jennifer stirred again and opened her eyes. She smiled a dopey grin.

"Hi," she whispered.

"Good morning Sleeping Beauty," Dr. Ortiz answered. "You're all done. Everything went very well. It looks good." Jennifer smiled.

"That's nice." She closed her eyes again. Dr. Ortiz stepped back from the bed.

"She'll be in and out for a while. I'll see her first

thing tomorrow morning and check her out."

"What time?" George asked.

"You can be here by ten." She started to leave.

"Is it really all-right, doctor?" Carol asked.

"From what I saw, yes. She'll be fine. You folks have a great Christmas...and don't worry."

The next morning Carol and George were at the hospital at nine o'clock. While Carol packed up Jennifer's things and arranged for a wheelchair to take her down to the front door, George went to pay the hospital bill. Jennifer, who worked as an account supervisor at Reiff Advertising, had medical insurance that covered everything except the TV and telephone. Neither had been used, but George had them installed in Jennifer's room anyway.

Doctor Ortiz caught up with Jennifer and Carol as they were boarding the elevator to the main floor. Jennifer was in n the wheelchair attended by an orderly.

"I thought you were going to wait for me," Dr. Ortiz said as the doors closed.

"I'm sorry," Jennifer answered. "I hate hospitals and I..."

"No problem," the doctor assured her. "I have

everything written out." She handed Carol the papers. "These are the prescriptions and instructions for the next few days. Bed rest today. Eat lightly. Take it easy." Carol watched Dr. Ortiz carefully while she listened. "Tomorrow you can do normal things. I'm sure you'll be your old self by Christmas Eve. Any problems, call me right away. I've left my service number, and my home number." The door opened onto the hospital lobby. The orderly wheeled Jennifer out first and headed for the main door. Carol stayed back with Dr. Ortiz.

"You're sure it's okay...I mean we have nothing to worry about."

"She'll be fine. If anything happens, or you have any questions, call me. I mean it. Everything looks fine, but surgery is surgery. Better safe than sorry. Okay?"

"Okay." Carol nodded. They caught up with Jennifer and the orderly.

"Thank you Alicia," Jennifer said. Dr. Ortiz put her hand on Jennifer's shoulder.

"Have a wonderful holiday."

"And when will you uh...want to see us?" Carol asked.

"The lab work will be back next Monday. You come in mid morning. I'll take out the stitches and we'll talk. And please, don't worry. Now I've got to go. Take care." She walked away briskly, as though on a mission.

"So where's Dad?" Jennifer asked as she got out of the wheelchair.

"Taking care of the bill for the TV and phone."

"Like I needed them."

"He wanted to do it," Carol said, looking around and feeling anxious to leave. She didn't like hospitals either.

George finished paying the cashier and headed toward the main lobby. He saw Dr. Ortiz coming toward him. He waved hello. She stopped.

"Good morning Mr. Boyajian. I just left Jenny and your wife in the lobby."

"Thanks. Look Doc... I know you said everything is okay and all that, but I know you send it... I mean the pathology people do give you an opinion right away, don't they?"

"Yes. While we're in surgery." Her expression tightened. Her lower lip slid under the upper.

"So what did they say?"

"It's inconclusive..."

"This is just me and you here now. I have to know." Dr. Ortiz saw the determination in George's eyes. She was not one to hide things or pull punches when patients prseed her for the truth.

"I'm afraid it wasn't good." George felt his knees weaken. He was shaken. Adrenaline coursed through his body. He felt a flush and struggled to stay composed. Dr. Ortiz noted his concern.

"It really is not conclusive. That's the truth. We'll know more after Christmas. Why don't you and the family go home and have a peaceful holiday? After that, we'll see... This is the 21st century. There's a lot we can do, Mr. Boyajian."

"Yes there is. Thank you for being up front with me." Dr. Ortiz nodded and started to leave.

"You uh...you didn't say anything to the women?"

"No. Not what I've just told you anyway."

George hurried to the lobby. On the way he decided not to say anything to Carol or Jenny about what Dr. Ortiz had told him. But now, more than ever, he was determined to try to make this holiday memorable for them. Somehow, Christmas had to happen for the Boyajian family again.

CHAPTER FIVE

'TIS THE SEASON

The next morning, just three days before Christmas Eve, George stood in the crowded lobby of the New Chatham Post Office. The overheated building caused him to perspire. It seemed as though everyone in town was sending off their Christmas gifts today. Being taller than most he could see that only one clerk station was open. It would take time to get waited on and he was impatient. Maybe he could come back later. He was about to leave when Tom Jennings appeared at one of the closed windows. He signaled for George to come over.

"I was on break when I saw you come in." Tom smiled, ignoring the daggers some of the patrons threw at him. His postal uniform was not as spit and polish as it was on Veteran's Day at the monument. "We waited on enough lines in the Army to last a lifetime, right, buddy?"

"That's for sure, Tom."

"What'll it be?"

"I'd like two books of Christmas stamps." A

quizzical look registered on Tom's face. He reached into the stamp drawer, but kept his eyes on George.

"I don't remember you buying Christmas stamps for a long time."

"Yeah. It's been a long time." George reached into his pocket, but Tom held up his hand.

"Let me get this," he said enthusiastically.

"Hey. No Tom. That's not necessary." Tom handed the two books of stamps to George.

"I know that. I want to. Just promise me you'll use one of them to send Lila and me a card." Tom reached in his pants pocket, retrieved a wad of bills, counted out the payment for the stamps, and placed the money in the till.

"That's a deal," George said, feeling the spirit of the season growing within him. It was something he had repressed for a very long time. "Thanks, pal."

"You're welcome. And have a real Merry Christmas."

As George stepped out of the post office he became aware that Christmas lights and decorations were everywhere. It was as if he was seeing it all for the first time. He felt a chill of excitement run down his spine. As he crossed the street, stepping out of the way of an oncoming pickup with a Christmas wreath fastened to its grill, Mayor Andy Lockwood waved to him from the other side. He was with his teenage son, Jason.

"Good morning, Andy...Jason," George said as he reached them. Andy was a widower. His wife had been killed in a plane crash in Texas, eleven years ago, while visiting her brother. The Mayor had never remarried, keeping busy with his legal practice, running the town, and raising Jason.

"Good morning, George," Lockwood responded. Jason nodded to George.

"And Merry Christmas," George said brightly. Andy Lockwood blinked with surprise. He had handled the Boyajian's affairs since they were married, and was acutely aware of the devastation John's death had caused to the family.

"Merry Christmas, Mister Boyajian," Jason said before his father could speak.

"Yes. Merry Christmas," the Mayor finally blurted out. "To Carol and Jenny too."

"Will do. See you later." There was a bounce of determination to George's step as he strolled down the street away from them. Andy Lockwood smiled and put his arm around Jason.

"I've waited too many years to hear that man say those words."

George paused at Williamson's Hardware window to admire the display of Christmas tree lights and ornaments stacked box upon box. He then took a deep breath and entered the store. Larry's grandfather, Joshua Williamson had started the business during the Roaring Twenties; Larry's father Rudy had run it during the prosperous war years and turned it over to his son a few years after Larry had returned from Vietnam. Larry had kept the old oak floor and cedar shelving, giving customers the feeling of shopping in the distant past... in a time when friendly service was the norm. He had added a few ramps and widened the aisles to accommodate his wheelchair. The shelves were packed with standard hardware items and signs announcing "Christmas Specials."

George found Larry Williamson patiently waiting on Miss Kearney. He waved hello.

"Be with you shortly, George. You know where everything is." Feeling like a teenage boy sneaking around to buy condoms in a drug store, George moved slowly, cautiously, toward a display of Christmas tree lights. Gingerly, he opened a thin cardboard box, removed a string of lights, and held them up for inspection. Larry rang up Miss Kearney's purchase while he kept one eye on George.

"Now there's a sight..." Larry muttered under his breath.

"How's that?" Miss Kearney asked. She was an attractive woman in her early forties – the New Chatham High School Guidance Counselor. The school was five miles to the south of downtown, although all the New Chatham's, East, West, and North, were slowly merging into one. Miss Kearney was divorced, and a relative newcomer to the area. At the moment she was quietly dating Andy Lockwood. It was "serious" according to the local gossip grapevine.

"George Boyajian's checking out the Christmas tree lights," Larry answered, not realizing she had actually heard him.

"Well Larry, people do buy Christmas tree lights at Christmas, don't they?" Larry returned his attention to Miss Kearney. "Huh? Oh yeah. Of course. Here's your change Miss Kearney. Merry Christmas."

"Merry Christmas. Say hello to Jan for me."

"Will do. And you wish Andy the same." She smiled and nodded. Larry watched her leave the store. He then turned his attention to George who had made his choice and now approached the cash register. With a sly grin on his face, George placed three boxes of modern Christmas lights on the counter.

"So? Replacing all your lights, George?"

"Sort of. Time to start fresh."

"I'm glad your women-folk finally..."

"Well Larry," George said in a conspiratorial tone, " Carol and Jenny don't actually know about my doing it yet. So if they..."

"I got it. It's tough. You know Jan still won't talk about her brother Dickie. Doesn't care to look at his name out there on our plaque either."

"Healing can take time for some," George said softly. Larry rubbed his paralyzed legs, an action he did absentmindedly when talk of Vietnam came up.

"Yes," Larry answered, his eyes averting George's. "I remember too much, too often..." Then he brightened quickly. "So? You guys are gonna have Christmas this year. That great!"

"I hope so. Jenny's with us this week. David, my grandson... he'll be here too. I'm gonna' try, Larry. If for nothing else, I want it for my Johnny." Larry nodded his agreement.

"You know, Johnny was the best after school clerk I ever had." Larry chuckled. "Did I ever tell you? One day, when he was workin' for me? we were tryin' to get this old chain saw fired up. She was seized, or something. I don't remember exactly. Anyway, I soaked her in oil. Finally kicked over, but she slipped. Lost my grip. Damned thing would have taken my useless legs off if Johnny hadn't knocked her out of the way. What reflexes! I don't know how the hell he did that without getting all cut up, but he did. You raised him right, George."

"I don't know. Sometimes I think maybe if I'd..."

"That kinda 'maybe if' don't work. What is, is. You know that better than most. Let it rest in peace." Larry carefully packed the Christmas lights in a white plastic bag. George pulled his wallet from his pocket. Larry handed the George the bag.

"Your money's no good here today, my friend. Merry Christmas."

"But..."

"No buts about it. I want to." He smiled. "I truly do, pal. Listen. You have a real special Christmas, George... You and the whole family. You guys deserve it." George took the bag and held it to his chest.

"Thanks Larry. You and Jan too." He started to leave, then turned back. "You know how you say you can still feel them sometimes? I mean your legs? Like they're working, but they're not?"

"Yeah. It happens. Like I can get up and run." Like before, he made a rubbing motion on his legs.

"Well, you know? I've had the weirdest feeling all day. It's like I can feel something I lost..." He touched his chest. "Here. Inside. It like it's really still there. Coming out to me. Like it isn't lost after all." Larry nodded and smiled. Great affection welled up inside him for his friend and comrade in arms.

"That's called Christmas, my good friend. And it was never lost. It can't be."

"Yeah....," George said wistfully. "I suppose you're right. Merry Christmas, Larry." He held up the package. "And thanks" George left carrying the lights and ornaments with his head held high. As George closed the door to the store behind him the tinny tinkling of the bell seemed to reaffirm the meaning and continuity of his life in this small town.

"God bless, pal," Larry said quietly to himself. "I wish you peace."

As George stood alone outside the store he gazed down Main Street, left and right. Many of the stores were different, many new people – but the lights and cold air and hustle of last minute shipping...it could have been fifteen years ago. He took a deep breath, allowing his eyes to go out of focus, and savored the moment.

"Mister Boyajian!" A tall, shapely woman in her thirties ran down the sidewalk toward George, waving. There was a cosmopolitan elegance to the casual way she was dressed in a pale blue car coat, with the pink collar of her blouse folded outside. She was no townie. Her faded Calvin Klein's showed the best of her figure – long, endless, legs. She thrust herself into George's arms causing him to nearly drop the bag of lights. Breathless, she hugged him, then back off, brushing away the long brown hair covering her face. George had a dumbfounded expression on his face.

"Oh dear. I've startled you," she said. He looked hard into the pretty face and eyes and found her.

"Elizabeth?" George said hesitatingly. She msiled broadly.

"Yes."

"My God. What are you doing here? I mean... I haven't seen you in... You're in Chicago, right?"

"Chicago. Married. Divorced. Isn't everyone?" she said flippantly, but disappointment was just underneath her smile.

"I'm not," he joked, trying to ease the moment.

"Of course not," she said, touching his arm. "You and Carol are my heroes." She looked around at the town.

"What brings you here?" he asked.

"The holidays. Something about home where the heart is I suppose. I'm staying with my Aunt Clara in South Chatham. My folks moved to Florida."

"Yes. I know. You going to stay?" She frowned.

"I'm going to give it a try. Are you finished with your shopping?" She glanced at his package.

"Huh? Oh...yes. I was heading for the station. Th town had grown but there's always parking down there." A private moment of recognition between them...the station and their last good-bye to John.

"I'll walk with you," she said. She took his arm. Her grip was firm and friendly as George and Elizabeth strolled down the Main Street toward the New York Central railroad station. After a few moments George experienced that feeling he had just described to Larry – the sensation that something buried and lost was reemerging. Elizabeth tightened her grip on his arm

"The fact is that I start this September at New Chatham High. Chemistry."

"That's wonderful. Welcome back." He patted her hand. "You were an engineer, right?"

"Petro-chemical. There was merger and I was tired of the travel and the hassles of being a woman around all those leering, sexist, oilmen...not to mention chauvinistic Arabs."

"I hear that. Well, their loss is our gain."

When they reached George's pickup he opened the door and placed the bag of lights and ornaments on the back seat next to other packages. They were gifts he had bought in earlier in the day. Elizabeth gazed down the station platform, as George did every time he was there. A memory imprinted. A first love lost.

"Hey, Elizabeth." She came out of her daydream, responding to his tone of voice. "You know after Johnny...and being Christmas and all that, we just stopped..."

"I know Mr. Boyajian. My Aunt said she heard that you still haven't celebrated Christmas...since John... Is that true?" He took her hand.

"It's George. And yes, that's true. But there are some things that you don't really know...can't know. But you can feel..." She nodded, fighting back tears. "So Elizabeth, I'm going to make a real effort to celebrate Christmas this year." Now the tears welled up in Elizabeth's eyes and flowed down her cheeks.

He gently pulled her to him, and comforted her with an embrace. "I know. I know. He wrote to me about it."

"We were going to announce it that Christmas. Oh, George... I still miss him so much. Some days, I feel like he's near – that he's about to come around the corner and into my arms. It's like he was never gone."

"Yes. For me too. Every day. Look dear, why don't you come by Christmas Eve for dinner? Jenny's home. Carol would love to see you..."

"I'd love to. But my Aunt's got her church thing. I don't go myself but she asked me to be with her."

"I understand." He was disappointed.

While George stood in the station parking lot with Elizabeth, Carol made her way to George's workshop. During their long marriage she and George had evolved rules that eventually became unspoken. Mostly, they defined boundaries and common interests. One was that George's workshop was his sanctuary - a place where he could work alone and undisturbed on projects for his customers, or himself. Carol had not been in George's workshop for a long time, but she knew what was there, and at this moment she was driven to see it...to hold it close.

The workshop, in the rear of a two story barn, had been converted for George's use. It was shaded by tall pines on the east wall and in summer, by a magnificent Oak to the south. Carol slowly turned the tarnished brass doorknob on the wide, pine-planked, double door, and pulled it open. She switched on the lights. Four large workbenches occupied much of the workshop. The walls were lined with tools hung on pegs. Table saws, band saws, and routers were on the workbenches. A variety of power tools, for almost every purpose imaginable, were spaced across the wide floor. In one corner of the shop, an enviable collection of 18th century tools were displayed and stored. Their condition attested to the fact that they were functional and in use. Carol smiled at the cleanliness of the workshop. She enjoyed the wood and varnish smell of it too.

Back in the far corner of the workshop was an ornate cabinet, which George had made years ago for his personal storage. Carol's intuition told her that what she was looking for would be in there. Her steps across the restored pine board floor sent out small, creaky echoes. Her sense of being an intruder was heightened by the stillness in the room. Through the windows she could see, but not hear, the pines swaying in the wind. It was as if she were watching a silent movie.

Her fingers trembled as she pulled on the ornate latch to the cabinet. Slowly the door swung open. She immediately caught sight of the dark brown edge of the frame. A slender shaft of light reflected off the frame's glass. With both hands she clutched it, then slowly removed it from the cabinet. Carol barely breathed. Her hands shook. She feared she might drop this treasure. Carefully, she placed it on one of the workbenches, and leaned over to examine it. Through the reflection of her face she gazed at the maroon velvet cloth, and the metal objects, neatly arranged before her.

Distinguished Service Cross. Air Medal. Purple Heart. Army Commendation Medal. Good Conduct Medal. National Defense Service Medal. Combat Infantryman's Badge. Southwest Asia Service Medal. Kuwait Liberation Medal.

Carol gasped, then clutched the frame to her breast. She had feared this moment, and yet was driven to experience it. Then, with eyes closed and heart pounding wildly, she relived Christmas Eve twelve years ago.

A sound came first - a car engine stopping at the top of the hill where the driveway made a deep descent toward the house. George had yet to plow the driveway. The winter had begun early and the accumulated snow was already three feet deep. She looked out of the living room window. There was snow was still falling heavily, like the perpetual white flakes in the crystal clear water of her snow globe. It would be a very white Christmas this year. She saw two uniformed Army officers trudging through the snow. The tall, well-tanned major, carrying a wide thin object, led the way. Next to him a shorter, paler man walked with his head down against the blowing snow. Speechless, she watched them leave trenches of white powder in their wake. The fear of who they were gripped her heart, her very soul. She silently prayed that they had the wrong house, and that when they got close enough to read the tarnished brass numbers on the door they would know it was all a mistake.

The first knock came. Carol did not move. A gentle rapping continued. Carol knew that in taking that first step to the door she was acknowledging their mission. Clutching the open neck of her blouse closed with one hand; she opened the door with the other. The harsh night wind blew a stream of snowflakes into the room. It rippled the pages of magazines lying on the coffee table. From the darkness, the taller man emerged into the weak light cast from the house.

"Mrs. Boyajian?" Carol nodded.

"I am Major Jeffers. This is Chaplain Moore."

"I... John...?"

"May we come in?" Carol nodded again, and shut the door behind the two officers who now stood nervously facing her. She felt their gaze and leaned against the door, with her face turned away from them, still clinging desperately to hope.

"Let me get my husband." Carol left the room with her hands held tightly to her face. She walked quickly through the living room and into the kitchen. Without pausing for a coat, she opened the back door and rushed out into the cold night. She ran through the snow to the workshop. When the shop door was flung open, it startled George, who was working intensely on a small, ornate chest.

"They're here, George!" The words choked in Carol's throat.

"What?"

"Two men... Army officers."

"Oh dear God," said George, dropping a

screwdriver from his right hand. "No!" He pushed the three legged stool he was sitting on out from under him and reached out for his wife, but she pushed him away.

"Go," she commanded. "You go first." George walked quickly toward the house, Carol following. Neither felt the chill of winter touch them.

The two officers were standing awkwardly in the living room when George and Carol arrived.

"Mister Boyajian, I'm Major Jeffers and this is Chaplain Moore."

"Sit down... Please," said George. Words choked him as they were squeezed from his throat.

"Thank you, sir." The two men sat on the couch. Carol took her husband's hand. They sat on a small love seat, facing the officers. The major took a deep breath, and then spoke calmly.

"I regret to inform you..." Carol moaned and sobbed. George clasped her hand. His cheeks twitched as tears filled his eyes, then coursed down his cheeks. *"...that your son, Staff Sergeant John Nelson Boyajian..."* Carol's shoulders quaked, and a mournful sigh rose from the depth of her soul. George put his arm around her and held her to his chest. *"...was killed in action against a hostile force*

on December twentieth, this year."

"Ohhh..." moaned George through his tears.

"He, and other members of the 5th Special Forces were on an operation in western Iraq. Their mission..." George looked at the major while he spoke. Carol remained curled against her husband, unwilling to look out at these messengers of death. "...their mission was to locate and target Iraqi Scud missile launchers." The Major took a deep breath and looked directly into George's eyes. "Their mission was a success, Sir. They located three launch sites. During the operation they came under heavy enemy fire. The Nightstalkers, the 160th Aviation Group, sent two Black Hawk helicopters to extract them. It was during this phase of the action that your son was killed."

"How?" George asked. Carol sat up. "Does it really matter, how?"

"How?" George insisted.

"Staff Sergeant Boyajian's team was climbing aboard the second Black Hawk. The hostile fire grew more intense and the team and the aircraft were in danger of being overrun. Sergeant Boyajian was climbing aboard when incoming fire killed the co-pilot and riddled the aircraft. All the rest of the team were aboard. According to the pilot, and your son's team members, Sergeant Boyajian waved for the pilot to lift off." Through his agony George felt a swell of pride. "He then grabbed the Squad Automatic Weapon from another soldier, and turned back toward the enemy, placing heavy fire into the oncoming hostile forces." The major's voice broke. He took a deep breath, and continued. "Mr. and Mrs. Boyajian, your son made a decision which saved the rest of his fellow soldiers at the price of his own life." George spoke through his tears.

"He died a hero."

"Yes sir, Mister Boyajian. Your son died a hero. He has been posthumously awarded the Distinguished Service Cross for his heroism." Carol got up. She glared at George, then the major, and finally, the still silent chaplain.

"Died a hero?" Her voice rose in volume and tenor, higher and louder. "Is that supposed to mean something to me, Major? Reverend? Are you here to tell me my son is in hero heaven? Is that supposed to comfort me?" And then, in a cold, heartless, disembodied voice she turned to George and said, "Why in God's name, did you let him do this?" She ran from the room, up the stairs, and slammed their bedroom door. George wiped the tears from his eyes. "She didn't mean..."

"I know, sir," the Chaplain said.

"We brought your son's decorations." The Major removed the brown paper wrapping from the framed display and ceremoniously offered it to George. He accepted the framed display, glancing quickly at the medals. He felt a moment of pride, but then looked upstairs toward the bedroom as Carol let out a wail of despair.

Remembering the depth and pain of her mournful cry brought Carol back to reality. She wiped the tears from her eyes, noticing some had dripped onto the glass. She took a corner of her blouse and wiped them too, and then replaced the case in the cabinet.

"Johnny," was all she could say, over and over, as she walked back to the house.

George drove home, parked in the driveway, and got out of the truck. He paused in the gathering dusk. Something was happening to him. Memories he rarely revisited these days were lining up like paratroopers on the ramp of a C-130. George just didn't know who the jump master was, or where the landing zone might be. Another night jump into the dark abyss of war. Staring at the distant hills, so peaceful on the winter dusk, he conjured F-4

Phantoms spewing thick trails of black exhaust in their wakes, as they came in low, dropping napalm that seared off the tops of hills along with those souls dwelling there. The fire and heat sucked away all the oxygen and life in its wake. George shook his head to remove those images of long ago and far away. This was his home. He was at peace even though the world was not and his town was considering adding more memorial plaques.

"My war...John's war...No end to this in sight," he told himself silently. "Madness." Then he walked toward the house. Carol watched him from the living room window.

"I know where you are, George Boyajian, and I know who you are," she said, whispering to herself. "Johnny wasn't your fault. He made his own choices. Not the ones I wanted for him. They were personal...like you did in your time."

As George walked toward the house he noticed Carol watching him from the window. She smiled and waved. Once inside, he took off his jacket and kissed her hello. She held his kiss longer than usual.

"I love you, George," she said when she finally released him. "I love you very deeply."

"And I've always loved you, Carol. As God is my witness...always." He embraced her and held her against his body for a long time. He breathed in the sweetness of her hair and the familiar scent of this woman who he loved and with whom he shared unbearable grief.

CHAPTER SIX

LIGHT A FIRE

The countryside was brown and bare. Winter's grip had hardened. All that grew and blossomed was now dormant. The sky above threatened. With the cold air, a snow storm felt imminent. The Boyajian farm, nestled on a hillock above the valley, was a Currier and Ives portrait without the snow, horse and sleigh, and joyous Christmas revelers.

It was Christmas Eve. As George split firewood next to the barn he had a view of the kitchen and noticed Carol working in there. Jennifer was settled into her old room and was resting. Her recovery from the surgery had been slower than anticipated, but David's arrival yesterday had cheered her immensely. There had been no further discussion about celebrating Christmas. Time was running out. He had his secretly bought presents for David, Jennifer, and Carol, hidden in the basement. The new lights were secreted in the attic underneath the old lights and ornaments. George paused in his labor and looked out across the wide, Chatham valley. Waist high stonewalls and narrow strips of asphalt connected the farms, villages, and towns of the valley. Behind the stonewalls, arrayed across the valley like so many points of bright yellow light, were the farmhouses of those hardy souls who remained to till the land. These were proud people, clinging tenaciously to their heritage. But keeping a small family farm in these days of mammoth farming corporations was a struggle. Yet somehow, several endured. George found their spirit uplifting as, in the face of adversity, they chose to stay with farming and their proud tradition.

Up and down the country lanes, green wreaths of evergreens, lacquered pinecones, and bright red ribbon, marked all the mailboxes - all except the Boyajian's. Throughout the county, families would be gathering tonight to decorate their Christmas trees with wooden angels, fishermen, camels, shiny and sparkling ornaments, glistening stars, tinsel, and strings of bright, cheery, blinking lights. Families together on Christmas Eve. Children eagerly anticipating their presents among peace and joy in the valley.

George ended his reverie and went back to work. The sound of the steel ax blade attacking the wood, and the clatter of the splits falling against an old stump that he used as a chopping block, echoed through the chilly air. Standing over the stump, wearing a green knit cap, a red and black Mackinaw, a faded pair of gray trousers, and knee high black rubber galoshes, George paused between swings of the ax. Long plumes of misty, hot breath rose from his mouth and spun a filmy cloud around his head. He leaned on the ax handle, then raised it high above his shoulder and brought it down in a swift, accurate arc into the log he had perched on the stump. The wood split in two with a crackling, breaking sound that meant it was dry and properly aged. George wiped sweat from his brow with the back of his wrist. He bent down to pick up the split and glanced at the old black plastic radio, spotted with a variety of paint - green, black, and white. He was tuned to a station playing non-stop Christmas carols and he realized with chilling clarity that the carol they were playing was "We Three Kings". A somber mood invaded his spirit like the cold wind that seeped through his Mackinaw. It assaulted his hold on the present with a memory of the past. John and he, singing that carol. It was their favorite. He frowned and shook it off.

"No, no, no," he said softly to himself and to the radio, as if he could banish the music that brought images and emotions of that terrible night so many years before. "Not tonight," he muttered. "Not again..." His gaze turned upward to the gray, overcast, sky. "Not tonight, Lord." Furtively he glanced down at the woodpile, and then toward the house. "Please!"

Carol stood in the warm, brightly lit, kitchen. She flipped the pages of a cookbook and found the recipe that she had remembered. Christmas Cookies. She was studying the ingredients so intently that she didn't hear Jennifer, in her socked feet, enter the room.

"Hi mom. What's up?" Carol was momentarily startled. She hurriedly closed the cookbook and slid it to the rear of the white tile counter.

"Oh. Hi, Honey. You're up early. Where's David?"

"Still sleeping. He was exhausted. The train being delayed took him way past his bedtime."

"But he had an adventure, now didn't he?" Jennifer poured herself some black coffee.

"I suppose. So what are you doing?"

"Me? Oh nothing. Just checking an old recipe. Did you have a good sleep?" Jennifer sat down at the kitchen table. She looked gaunt and tense.

"I can't stop thinking about... David is so worried that I'm going to... I mean what if..." Carol sat down at the kitchen table next to Jennifer.

"What ifs can eat you alive. You need to be patient. And positive. We'll know Monday, and then we'll know what we have to do." Carol stroked Jennifer's hand.

"Dad sure seems busy," Jennifer said, not wanting to discuss it further. "And happy. I heard him singing along with some carols before when he was stacking the logs."

"He's up to something."

"How can you tell?"

"After all these years?" she smiled knowingly, "I can tell. He gets this funny little-boy look."

"He wished David and me Merry Christmas last night. I haven't heard that from him for...I can't remember."

"He cleaned out the basement yesterday. I've been after him to do that for months." Carol looked out the window. She watched George swinging the long-handle ax with the ease of a young man. Hoe she loved him! The stack of firewood was growing.

"Now he's out there chopping wood like a kid. He's still strong as an ox, but he's not a kid, you know." Carol turned back to her daughter. "He said it's going to snow. Are you hungry sweetheart?"

"No." Jennifer winced as disconcerting pain she had grown familiar with shot across her back. Carol noticed.

"What is it?" Jennifer got up. When the pain occurred she needed to walk it off.

"It's the stitches," she lied. "I just need to walk a little. It's nothing."

"I'll go with you."

"No," she said quickly, then smiled. "I mean thanks mom. I'd like to be alone for a while." Jennifer left the room. A deep sadness overcame Carol. She sat down. Her only surviving child in pain...and the possibility of... No! She didn't want to think about it. But it would not leave her. 'I buried one child. To have another... No!' She closed her eyes tightly and shuddered. 'No! God no! That would kill me.' The sound of the ax biting into wood distracted her. She walked to the kitchen door and opened it. The cold air and the sight of her husband swinging the ax with precision and rhythm cleared away the terrible thoughts. Her heart filled with love for him. Driving away her fears. This was her man, her special man, with whom she had shared so much...a life. Then, as she turned to close the door, she noticed a tarnished brass hook. Carol reached out and gently touched it. Time and space melted as the sound of the ax chewing wood became the click of a hammer on brass...

Carol saw a younger George with a teenage John, and seven year old Jennifer, standing by the door. The children watched as George finished gently nailing the brass hook, bright and polished, onto the door. He then gestured for John to pass him the full, rich decorated Christmas wreath, and hung it on the hook. George lifted Jennifer so that she could attach the bright red bow she had made in school. The family all admired the wreath. There was no doubt it announced the season beautifully. And the kids loved it.

Then a gust of wind faded the memory and Carol went back, alone, into the kitchen and her troubles.

George turned off the radio. He looked up as the first snowflakes began to flutter to earth. A few drifted onto his eyelashes and melted, becoming unwarranted tears. He smiled and wiped the sweat from his forehead.

"Perfect," he said aloud. "A white Christmas. The season begins. Our daughter and grandson are here..." He conversed with himself to build his courage. He conspired. "A nice fire will warm them up. I've got to try, don't I?" He swung the ax and split a final log. The pieces flew into the air, catapulted from bondage to freedom. George paused, his labor done. He allowed the now heavier snowflakes to gather on the back of his leather work gloves. In seconds they were coated in white crystals. Reverently, George raised a glove to his face. He pressed the cold, virgin snow against his overheated flesh. Then slapping his hands together, George picked up a stack of cordwood. "We've mourned enough," he whispered, more as a prayer than a statement of fact as he walked up the gentle slope toward the house. He glanced up at Jennifer's room. He thought about her divorce, her illness, his grandson's fears, Johnny, dear Johnny gone. Life had dealt some hard blows. Now he had to do something to lift them all up.

"Daddy's coming with wood," Jennifer announced as she came back into the kitchen. "And it's beginning to snow.

"A fire would be nice," Carol said, setting aside

the cookbook again.

"A white Christmas," Jennifer whispered. Carol changed the subject.

"Are you feeling better dear?" Jennifer started to cry again.

"I don't know what I'm going to do. I feel like time is running out. It's so unfair to David. To me." Carol embraced her daughter.

"We don't know that's the case, now do we?"

"We take so much for granted until..." Jennifer looked at her mother. "I was thinking about Harold. Maybe if I'd tried harder we'd still be married and..." Carol stroked her daughter's hair.

"That's foolish talk! You tried harder than anyone I know to make your marriage work. He wasn't going to grow up, and that was that." Jennifer pulled away from Carol's embrace.

"I don't know what you mean, "grow up.""

"It doesn't matter. Look. You've got to keep fighting. We all do."

"I don't know if I can...if I have the strength."

"Of course you do. Now you listen to me. It's going to be okay. You hear me? I feel it in my bones." She hugged Jennifer again.

George stood quietly in the doorway as he

observed his wife and daughter's private moment. He then opened the kitchen door and backed in, carrying the split wood.   He stamped his feet, depositing small chunks of mud and ice on the doormat. He then faked staggering under the burden of the wood.

"Oh daddy, close the door," Jennifer called out. "It's freezing!" George kicked the door closed and headed for the living room, still feigning the strain of the load. He conjured up his best Scottish accent.

"Ach, now lassies - a harsh and cruel Winter it is. Not a fit night out for man nor beast." George went directly to the living room fireplace and dropped the logs onto the slate hearth. He laughed, and gestured to the women as if he were showing respect to royalty. "Hoot-mon, me bonnie lassies, soon t'will be warmth and the cheer of Christmas in our humble castle." George knelt at the fireplace, slid opened the metal, mesh curtain, and began to stack the logs onto a seasoned pair of brass andirons. He sneaked a glance over his shoulder, noting that neither woman had reacted to his mention of Christmas. George studiously cleared his throat.

"Carol? Jennifer?" He waited until he had their attention. "I've been thinking."

"That's always dangerous," Carol said jokingly.

She smiled nervously at Jennifer.

"All these years we've..."

"Let's not start that again, George," Carol said, cutting him off. George rose to his feet.

"Neither was wasting our son's life."
Carol's voice cut, hard and bitter. George walked to her side. Jennifer watched them both intensely.

"Is that what you really think? That his life was wasted?"

"Not all the time. But now... My God George, we're at war again in that same horrible place. And this time we're alone. They're talking about staying to 'finish the job'... Iraq, Afghanistan, who knows where else. What did Johnny's death in that damned desert accomplish anyway? What did it make better? We lost a son, and for what? An unfinished job? Can you tell me for what? Can you tell me?"

"I can't. I...I don't know." George looked at John's photograph again, as if he were speaking to him.

"How many boys like John do they want? Who made us the world's policemen? Why is always old men whose sons are not in harm's way making those decisions?" Carol's anger about her son's death had come to the surface often in those first few years.

Then, as time passed, she seemed to have controlled it. But as the bodies or young American men and women began to come home from the second Iraq War it bubbled up again with a vehemence that was visceral. In the past George had defended the action of his government. But now he wasn't sure why they were at war.

"I used to think it was about America and democracy and freedom. But now...I don't know dear. It was something we grew up with. Something that was part of our life. We accepted defending freedom as an American responsibility. Maybe it's changed. I don't know. I just don't know anymore." Carol sat down.

"So what's the point of it all?"

"I know that I loved...that I love my son, and that I miss him every day of my life. I believe John knows that having Christmas doesn't mean we forgot him." Jennifer and Carol were both teary. Carol held up her hand to stop him.

"Please George..." He went on anyway, determined to have his say.

"I believe that having Christmas for the first time since... well, I believe that somehow he'll know. Somehow, he needs to know. We owe him that. We owe ourselves and our family that. We do. We surely do." There was a long silence.

"Maybe daddy's right," Jennifer finally said, struggling to control her emotions. "Maybe it's time to close... to find a way to end the pain."

"Sure I'm right. You'll see, Jenny..." But Carol's attitude hardened.

"So it's that easy, huh? You snap your finger and our pain goes away? Celebrate Christmas and all's well! All these years this season never existed, and now, suddenly this Christmas, everything is different?" This kind of anger was something that she rarely showed in front of Jennifer.

"Maybe because this well might be my last Christmas," Jennifer said quietly. There was an air of hopelessness in her voice. Carol came quickly to her daughter's side.

"What is wrong with you, George?"

"I only want to..." Carol cut him off.

"Let it go. This child needs her family now... Not ghosts." George watched Jennifer run up the stairs to her room. Carol threw him an angry look and went into the kitchen. "Sometimes I just don't understand you," she said, closing the kitchen door behind her. He turned to the cold fireplace, opened the flue, and prepared to start a fire. Half-formed thoughts filled his mind, and then slipped away, unable to emerge. He struggled to find words to convince Carol that he was right. Methodically, as if to buy time, he stacked the fresh split wood on the andirons, then reached to a nearby wicker basket and removed some old newspapers. The only sound in the room was his crushing the newspaper into small balls. Then he heard a clatter of small feet coming down the stairs.

In David's eyes his grandfather knew all, had done all, and was the fountainhead of knowledge, fun, and unconditional love. The boy lit up George's life. He didn't know how many more years their relationship would remain this way, so he'd vowed to himself to enjoy every moment that the two had together.

"Grandpa!" David shouted as he burst into the room. The boy was barefoot, still wearing his pajamas with the colorful action heroes printed on them. Atop his sleep-matted, brown hair, David wore John's desert camouflage hat. In his right hand he held a photograph of John taken when he'd completed his Special Forces training.

Carol came out of the kitchen. She knelt down and kissed David on the forehead.

"Good morning, sleepyhead. How about some breakfast?"

David had other things on his mind. Carol understood when she noticed the photograph in his small hands.

"Grandpa, tell me about Uncle John. And the Army," the boy asked as he crossed the room to George. Carol saw what was coming and backed away. The past few years, since Carol and Harold divorced, David had been obsessed by the life of the uncle he never knew. George glanced at Carol. Her expression reflected the pain that mention of John and the army conjured up. 'Out of the mouths of babes,' George's expression seemed to say to her. 'What can I do?' George took David's hand and led him to the sofa. They both sat down. George took John's photograph and placed it on the nearby coffee table facing them.

"I want to be a soldier like Uncle John," David announced. It was not a new idea.

"You know, David, this is a hard thing to talk about."

"Why?"

"Well, it's sort of a grown up thing and you're young. You haven't had many experiences."

"I had one last night on the train, Grandpa, when it was late." George smiled at David's grasp of things.

"And I wasn't worried or scared. I knew you would wait for me." George put his arm around his grandson.

"Yes. But there are some things that are more scary, and perhaps difficult for you to understand."

"I don't know what you mean," the boy said as he looked directly into his grandfather's eyes. It was clear that he had a need to hear about the uncle he only knew as a hero, according to his mother.

"Soldiers die in war. Have you ever seen anyone die?"

"On TV... And in the movies."

"That isn't real. Those are actors, and make up, and special effects."

"I know it's make believe, Grandpa."

"Okay."

"But you were in a war," David said.

"Yes. I was. What I'm trying to say is that it's tough to talk to someone young, who hasn't been there, about what it's like. It's even hard for most grown-ups to imagine if they weren't there."

"So I'll go there and then I'll know too." George was frustrated and at the same time proud of how bright and determined David was.

"Let's try this. What's the worst thing you can imagine?"

"The worst thing?"

"Yes. Of anything that could happen to you, what would be the worst?"

"If mommy, and you, and Grandma died... And daddy too. I'd be all alone."

"Now...imagine if that happened and all the Grandmas and Grandpas and mommies and daddies in the whole town were killed in one day by bad men." George watched David's brow furrow as the young boy's mind grappled with this image.

"That's pretty bad. And no one would be left?"

"No one. That's something like what a war can be...when everyone you know is gone."

"I know," he said brightly. "Like all the people in the World Trade Center when the terrorists killed them?"

"Yes," said George. "Like that." He sat up and faced David. "Now... let's make a pact."

"What's a pact?" George took David's hand.

"It's a solemn oath between you and me."

"Do I have to raise my right hand?" George smiled. "No. I'll take your word for it. Here's the oath."

David listened intently and George knew this was something his grandson would never forget. He weighed his words carefully and spoke slowly and clearly.

"If you still want to join the Army when you're older, say nineteen or twenty, first you come up here to the farm and you and I will spend a few days together. I'll tell you everything I can remember about war. I'll tell you, as best I can, what it's really like. Then, if you still want to go, at least you'll have some idea of what you might encounter. Movies and TV and the news can't prepare you. But maybe I can. So do we have a pact?" George extended his hand. David took it. They shook hands.

"Pact," said David with a wide grin. He felt grown up, having this new bond between himself and his grandpa.

"Now...about your Uncle John. He decided to join the Army. He wanted to serve and defend our country by fighting against the bad men. He chose to join one of the most elite units in the Army."

"What's elite?"

"Special. They are actually called Special Forces. Many men try to join, but only a few get through all the training and tests. It's very hard and demanding. You've got to be tough. Tough and smart."

"That's what I want to be – Special Forces."

"First you learn infantry, then how to parachute out of planes..." David's eyes lit up.

"That is soooo cool, Grandpa."

"Cool?" He smiled. "I suppose it is. Then your Uncle John went to Ranger School."

"Ranger School? Is that more tests?"

"Sort of. It's where the best of the best go for more training. Rangers learn to fight anywhere in the world; mountains; forests; swamps; snow... the desert..."

"Mommy told me that Uncle John was killed in the desert."

"Yes he was."

"My Uncle John was tough and smart."

"That he was. And after Ranger School he was accepted by the Special Forces." David's eye's lit up.

"Hey, I know them. The Green Berets."

"Right. Your Uncle John was a light weapons expert. He could train anyone, anywhere, to use light weapons."

"What are light weapons?"

"Rifles, pistols, machine guns, some rocket launchers."

"Wow."

"And he was also trained as a medic so he could take care of the other soldiers who might get hurt."

"So that means my Uncle John could fight the bad guys and save the good ones."

"Exactly," George said softly. He wiped a tear away before it could fall. But David was sharp and caught the action.

"Are you crying, Grandpa?" George took a deep breath and touched David's downy cheek.

"It's hard for me to talk about Uncle John."

"But he was a hero."

"Yes. He was. But he was also my son, and I miss him very much, and I wish he were here." George had not noticed that throughout his conversation with David, Carol had been standing at the kitchen door, listening. "He was a hero in many ways. He volunteered to serve his country. He went through all the struggle and hardship to be part of Special Forces." George felt pain and equally fierce pride surge within him. "And on the last day of his life, your Uncle John made a choice. He chose to save his buddies by giving up his own life. That's why he is a hero." George reached out and held David to his chest. He didn't want the boy to see him crying, but he could not help himself. And then Carol was at George's side as she sat down on the couch.

"Why is Grandpa crying?"

"Because," Carol asnwered, "he loved your Uncle John, and misses him very much. We all do." The phone rang. George wiped his eyes on his sleeve and released David. He got up and walked to the kitchen to answer the phone.

"Hello."

"George? Hi there. It's uh, Harold." His ex son-in-law sounded tentative, as if he expected the cold shoulder. But at this moment George was of another mind.

"Merry Christmas, Harold."

"Uh, yeah. Merry Christmas, George. How are you? How's mom?"

"We're all fine."

"David got in okay?"

"Yes. The train was late, but he handled it like a trooper." George smiled to himself at his choice of words.

"Good. Listen... Can I, uh, speak to Jennifer?" Carol and David came into the kitchen to get some breakfast. George placed his hand over the receiver. "It's Harold," he told Carol. "He wants to speak to Jennifer."

"Is that my daddy?" David blurted out. "Can I speak to him?" George handed the phone to David.

"Daddy? It's snowing. I had an adventure on the train last night." George could not hear what Harold said to his son, but after what Jennifer had said about the argument on Thanksgiving, he was glad to see that David bore no grudge. "Are you coming to Grandma and Grandpa's?" David asked. George looked at Carol.

"What should we do?" he mouthed silently.

"It's between them," Carol said softly. "I'll tell Jennifer he's on the phone." She went upstairs while David continued to talk to his father about the train ride, and how it was beginning to snow. Not wanting to distract David, George went back to the living room to light a fire.

CHAPTER SEVEN

TAKE A CHANCE

An hour later George stood at the living room window and watched as the snow thickened and covered the land and trees in a shroud of white. Flakes floated by, stuck together as though a huge, cosmic, pillow fight had broken out above. It was getting toward evening, and the cloudy sky hurried the fading light. In this silent, peaceful moment, a small herd of deer emerged at the edge of the woods. They foraged, poking their sharp hooves down through the new blanket of snow to the brown grass below.

Carol sat on the sofa in front of the fireplace, reading a book to David. The fire was now warm and steady, with a red and blue hot coal bed. With a deep exhale George turned and slowly ascended the stairs. He was aware of the slight give of the thick pile carpet beneath his shoes. One edge now, his senses were heightened. He reached the upstairs hallway and walked to Jennifer's room. George listened at the door for a moment, then knocked.

"Yes?" Jennifer's voice was calm and awake.

"Can I come in Jenny?"

"Sure dad." George opened the door slowly, respectfully. Jennifer was lying on her bed in the darkened room. He sat on the bedside and took her hand in his with a comforting touch.

"How're you doing baby?"

"Fine, daddy." After her conversation with Harold she had gone back up to her room without comment.

"Everything okay with Harold?" George tried to be as casual as he could.

"He wanted to come up. I guess he's feeling a little guilty or something?"

"Guilty?"

"Not being with me at the hospital. He did ask, but I didn't... And then...well, you know... see I didn't tell you guys everything about the argument we had on Thanksgiving. David overheard and got angry and physical wit Harold. In his mind he was trying to defend me, and I didn't explain...I mean how can I to a child? I was angry too. It all really upset Harold."

"That's too bad."

"Well, thankfully kids are kids. David got over

it. They talked it out."

"Is he coming up?"

"I told him not to." George was disappointed.

"I understand. It's just for David and Christmas it might..."

"I'm sorry, Dad. I know you want to have Christmas so

much. I want it for David too. But I just... And it's not about Johnny. It's me and this lousy situation..." George squeezed her hand gently.

"I wish I could take away your pain...And your illness. I can't really know what you're going through. I do know about uncertainly. If I could absorb it all, I would." He lifted her hand to his mouth and kissed it.

"Thank you," she said. "I love you, daddy."

"I know. And we love you with all..." He looked into her eyes. "I've wanted to tell you what happened to me at the monument that night. Something extraordinary. And after, I got this feeling...a really good feeling...and Johnny seemed to..." Jennifer frowned. Her world was steeped in harsh reality; while here he was, talking about ephemeral events. He held up his hand. "Okay. Here's the thing. I'm asking you to give me this one night. One Christmas Eve. Is that so much?" Jennifer's response was a strong squeeze of George's hand. He leaned over and gently kissed her on the forehead, then left. Jennifer closed her eyes. Her thoughts drifted to a day in High School.

She was in Mrs. Walker's senior English class at the New Chatham High School. It was a year after John's death. Christmas decorations were displayed on the classroom windows and walls. While Jennifer sat quietly at her desk, the other kids chatted noisily about the Christmas break and their plans for skiing in the mountains, tanning on a Caribbean beach, or gathering with family in some distant, exciting place like New York City. The discussions swirled around Jennifer like a tornado, pulling her in every direction. She could hear Claire Patterson describing how much fun her New Year's party would be, and how happy she was that her boyfriend was returning home from his first semester at college. Bobbie Hutchens showed off her stylish haircut that would fit in with the Broadway show crowd, and Brianna Crowley poured out her joy at having her braces off for good by Christmas.

But for Jennifer it was another year without her big brother John and without Christmas. Just an unhappy time when her parents hardly spoke – a silence in the house that she dreaded; a deep sorrow that permeated her home. The other students had learned, and understood, how sensitive Jennifer was to the mention of Christmas, or her brother's death. But this clique of girls was insensitive, or maybe just being girls. There were other kids, unable to console her, who respectfully kept their distance and their silence.

In the corner of the classroom, Mrs. Walker kept a concerned eye on Jennifer. The news was full of High school suicides seemed to be occurring at epidemic rates, especially during the holiday season. Jennifer Boyajian seemed to reflect several of the classic symptoms and it trouble her teacher. When she thought Jennifer was not watching, Mrs. Walker went over to Claire, Bobbi and Brianna and holding h3er voice to a whisper, chided them for being insensitive toward Jennifer. But Jenny heard her, and although the girls stopped their talk, she was embarrassed and felt singled out from the rest of the class. She was never friendly with those three girls again.

A while later, when George came back

downstairs, Carol was still reading to David. It was a book about a boy who wanted to be an astronaut. Carol looked up from the book as he came into the living room.

"How is she?"

"Okay," George said. He stoked the fire, then sat down on the couch and put his arm around her. "So here's the plan. I've brought the new lights and ornaments down to the den along with the boxes of old ones. You and the guys can start to sort them. I'll go get a tree..." George felt Carol stiffen. David nearly flew off the sofa with excitement.

"A tree!" he shouted. "And lights!" Carol was sandbagged. She was about to unload on her husband when she saw the joy on her grandson's face. She glared at George. He winked at her and then kissed her lips lightly, but with great tenderness. It was a kiss that means we are together forever.

"I just don't understand how you can do such an about-face after all these years," she said after David had run into the den to inspect the boxes.

"You have to trust in me." The clock on the mantel chimed five times. Carol shivered and glanced toward the front door as if she had heard the bell ring.

"It was just about this time..." George held her

close. She was stiff in his arms, and shaking.

"It was long ago. This is the right thing to do now. Please." She breathed deeply. He felt her body relax. He shoulders sagged against him.

"I'm not promising anything," she sighed.

"I am."

"And that is?"

"Healing." Carol looked deeply into his eyes, more with love than passion; more with hope than sorrow. He held her face in his, roughly callused hands. "Thank you." And then he was up and filled with the energy she had always loved him for. "Now!" he pronounced. "Let's get the ornaments and lights in here. David!" he called out. "Go upstairs and tell your mother what's up. Then come help Grandma." The boy rushed to the task, eager to begin making Christmas.

A short while later, the living room sofa, chairs, and coffee table were covered with an eclectic collection of Christmas tree lights and ornaments that had not seen the light of day for more than thirteen years. Carol supervised David as they sorted through them like treasure hunters who had come upon a huge cache of goodies. Jennifer was still upstairs, showering. George came into the room as he slipped into his heavy blue, yellow, and red, plaid mackinaw.

"At this late hour we'll probably wind up with the tree from hell, if one at all," George observed sarcastically.

"Then it'll be special," Carol answered, now trying to play along with his enthusiasm, as much for David and Jennifer as for herself. "And if there are none, you'll just have to get your ax and flashlight and go into the woods."

"Right you are, boss. Oh...into the woods of Grandmother's house to find a tree we'll go," George sang off key to David.

"That's Little Red Riding Hood,' David observed. "I played the wolf once in school." George leaned toward his grandson and made a funny face.

"And were you a mean wolf?" David laughed.

"No Grandpa. I was a funny wolf."

"I love you, funny wolf," he said, pulling him up into his arms. Then he put David back down among the ornaments and lights. "And now I'm off – a man on a mission!" He planted a loving kiss deep in the crook of Carol's neck that gave her chills. "Keep the home fires burning boys and girls, and a light in the window that I may find my way home."

Get a full one," Carol reminded him.

"Right," George answered.   He was a kid, charged with excitement for fuel.

"And a stand," she added. "One with a pan for water."

Ten minutes later, Jennifer, who felt refreshed and relaxed after a hot shower, slowly descended the steps to the living room. She looked around at the lights and ornaments.

"Wasting no time, huh?" David jumped up and ran to her.

"Look! We're really having Christmas mommy! Grandpa's getting a tree and everything..." The glow on his face, and excitement in his voice, removed any lingering opposition that either woman had to George's plan.

"How do you feel, dear?" Carol asked.

"Pretty good...for the first time in along time."

"Want to help sort all this out?"

"Yes, mommy. Help us," David begged. "There's a lot of stuff here. And Grandpa got new lights too."

"Where's dad?"

"Gone to get tree."

"A full one," David added. "Can you help us mommy?"

"Sire. But maybe I'll have a bite to eat first."

"There's ham and cheese in the fridge. And you can warm the chicken broth in the blue container. Carol took Jennifer's appetite as a hopeful sign. They would know for certain in a few days.

When Jennifer returned from the kitchen she carried a cup of coffee and a plate of Oreo cookies. She found David totally immersed in sorting out ornaments by color and size. Carol was at the living room window watching the snow accumulate. Jennifer joined her there.

"Cookie?" she asked, offering the plate to her mother. Carol smiled.

"Oreo's, huh? Did you scrape out the icing?" It was reference to one of Jennifer's habits where she would open the package of the crème filled cookies, separate the chocolate halves, scrape out most of the white icing, leaving just enough to paste the halves back together and put them back in the box. Jennifer laughed.

"No. I forgot." She laughed too. Carol took a cookie.

"It's beautiful out. A white Christmas." Both women looked back at David who was totally absorbed in sorting out the ornaments.

"He's so excited," Jennifer said.

"So is your father."

"Just like you said - a little boy." She glanced back at David. "Two little boys."

"Filled with hope. He was that way with Johnny. They were more like playmates than father and son."

"I sort of remember that."

"Dad thinks some kind of Christmas magic will make everything right."

"And you? What do you think, mom?" Jennifer looked at her mother with a somber expression.

"I can't imagine feeling differently." Jennifer watched the snow falling for a moment. She sipped her coffee.

"You know mom, I never told you guys, but all those years with no Christmas was a sort of hell for me." Startled by Jennifer's words, Carol turned to face her. "The kids at school would talk about what they got...about their families gathering...trips over vacation trimming the tree...all about their Christmas'. I would see the whole town celebrating. And I had this notion that we didn't have Christmas because..." she paused as if to be sure to chose her words carefully, "...because you loved Johnny more than me." Carol felt her heart sink. She closed her eyes, feeling her daughter's pain and her own shame.

"Oh..." was all she could manage.

"I was convinced I didn't deserve a Christmas because he wasn't there." Carol, stunned by this revelation, pulled Jennifer to her breast, spilling the coffee and cookies on the floor. She ignored them.

"Oh no! No dearest! Oh! I'm so sorry." Carol cried and Jennifer felt a strange relief in her mother's arms. "Did you really think that?" All Jennifer could do was nod affirmatively against her mother's swaying shoulder. She was too choked to speak.

"No! No! We love you both... Equally." She looked into Jennifer's eyes. "Oh dear God. We were just so consumed with grief, we didn't..." Carol saw clearly there was no getting around the pain they had caused their daughter all these years. "There is no excuse, is there? Oh my dear God...what have we done?" Jennifer knelt down an began to pick up the coffee mug, plate and cookies. Carol knelt next to her and took her hand. "We are such fools. Can you ever forgive us?"

"I have, mom." They both looked toward David and the lights and ornaments. He was totally absorbed and had not noticed what transpired. From this point of view, with the fire behind them, the ornaments sparkled and twinkled with a cheery orange light. David looked like an angel seated among them.

"Maybe your father's right about having Christmas again. Maybe it is time to look ahead. Let's get started."

At that same moment, Harold, struggling with three huge Saks Fifth Avenue shopping bags that were bulging with gift wrapped presents, was swept along with the crowd entering Grand Central Station. Sweat beaded on his forehead, and soaked his shirt underneath his heavy winter coat. College students cutting it close to get home in time for Christmas Eve; stalwart businessmen putting in a long last day before the holiday; soldiers, sailors, and marines on leave; and last minute shoppers now heading for the suburbs, constituted the holiday throng. Harold felt excitement, and holiday cheer, emanating from these people. He could smell another kind of cheer on some of their breaths which made him consider a quick stop at Charlie Brown's. But hr thought better of it. As he jostled with the crowd, images of what Christmas was supposed to be like, filled his senses; 'It's A Wonderful Life' - God, how many times Jennifer could watch that each Christmas; 'Amal and the Night Visitors' – a favorite of David's because it was about a young boy; The Mormon Tabernacle Choir, and the Harlem Boy's

Choir - all presenting uplifting emotions that we were supposed to feel. And yet, life somehow never quite attained what those onscreen characters found, or the music promised. These days it all seemed to make things worse. He concluded that anticipation never measures up to the reality. But today, more than ever, he wished it might. Something important had surfaced in his life. Something had changed.

Harold finally reached the train and saw that the rear cars were packed. He headed down the platform toward the front where the head cars were past the platform's end. He stepped up the narrow steel steps into the last car accessible from the platform, then walked forward through two more cars, and finally found seats in the head car. Harold stacked his packages and the overnight bag he'd packed in the storage rack above, then collapsed in an empty seat. As the car filled quickly, he retrieved his cell phone from his jacket pocket, flipped the black plastic lid open, and began to dial the Boyajian's. Then he decided against it, and flipped the phone shut. 'If I call now,' he reasoned, 'she can say don't come. But if I just show up, that will mean something. And it'll be tough for them to send me away.' His heart raced at the thought of what had now become incredibly important to him – Jen and David. His family. His life was not designer shoes; Armani suits; monogrammed shirts; a Mont Blanc pen; Italian frames; or the Rolex Oyster on his wrist. Picturing all that as important made him chuckle aloud. Nearby passengers eyed him for drunk. Harold's entire life was a carefully constructed image, facing outward to the world - clothes, hair styling, doctored resume, the "right" clubs and social groups. He had created an image for success and a means to attain what he believed everyone else wanted. He had lied to himself. It had all crystallized in Callihan's bar when his "lady" had just stopped by to give her husband a kiss. It was love. Harold loved his wife and child. The shock of being alone was unacceptable. It was wrong. He didn't want to be alone anymore. The sensation was overpowering. But was he going back to Carol, and David, out of weakness? not love? Was he merely tricked by the current barrage of Christmas sentiment?, or did he truly, deeply, want his family above all else? He thought back again to bar and the conversation he'd had with Danny Callahan after his wife left. Yes. There as no doubt. 'You'll do the right thing,' Danny said. He knew what that was now, and he would try. For above all, he wanted was his family back... Whatever it took.

Harold closed his eyes, exhausted from his quest for gifts and the rush to the train. He settled back in his seat as the train lurched forward and slowly made its way out of the underground cavern of Grand Central Station toward the gathering winter night. He listened to the clacking and squealing of steel wheels against steel track. He found comfort in the sounds, and rocking, cradling motion of the train. It was taking him to his family...to people he needed, and who, he prayed, still needed him. He stuffed his ticket into the leather slot on the seat in front of him where the conductor would find it. Then he fell into a deep sleep for an hour, not noticing the stops the train made, nor the passenger who got on or off.

When Harold awoke it was dark outside, and snowing. He had no idea where they were. He rubbed his eyes and stretched sitting down, flexing his back and leg muscles. It felt good. He looked around the overheated car. Across the aisle he noticed an old woman wearing pearls, a faded but serviceable black dress, pumps, and an old Fox coat draped around her shoulders. She seemed to have made an attempt to dress up. He wondered briefly where she was going, and who was going to meet her. The holidays seemed to set everyone one motion, either rushing from something, or to something, or chasing dreams that someone once told you happened at this time of year. The commuters that had been on the train when it left Grand Central were mostly gone now, replaced by longer distance travelers. Valises, backpacks, and gift packages had replaced attaché cases and dress coats on the overhead racks. He saw his ticket had been punched. And then he tasted the sticky, pungent odor in mouth and wanted a drink. As her got up he noticed the occupants in the row in front of him were a young mother in her late twenties with a toddler, exhausted from the day's activities, and an infant whom the mother nursed under a discrete cover. To Harold, it was a comforting sight mixed with an unhealthy dose of guilt over his own family.

The bar car was fairly crowded, but he lucked out with timing and got a seat just as a young couple got up. He seated in and noted the bartender was busy. While waiting Harold toyed with the idea of calling New Chatham again but reached he same conclusion as before - if he called now Jenny could say don't come.

"Excuse me, sir," a voice said behind him. "Is

this seat taken?" The voice belonged to a soldier in his late forties or early fifties. Glancing sideways Harold could make out five rows of ribbons and shiny silver insignia affixed to the dark green uniform. Short, gold bars, at least ten of them, were sewn to the right sleeve of his uniform jacket, and miniature gold stripes were sewn to his left sleeve. In mid-arm was a sergeant's rank insignia that Harold was not familiar with – three stripes on top, three below in a rocker, and a gold diamond in the center. Though Harold had no comprehension of the significance of the soldier's decorations or insignia, the cumulative effect was that this man had been in the army for a while and had done a lot.

"Uh, no. Not at all." The soldier sat down. 'Sir? Him calling me sir.' Harold thought.

"Do you mind if I smoke?" the soldier asked.

"Not at all." A Zipppo illuminated the sergeant's face in the dimly lit bar car, the yellow glow highlighting the lines and one lip to temple scar on the man's face. Harold had a passing thought that tried to imagine what Carol's brother John looked like in uniform. The old questions that gnawed at him when Jennifer spoke of her brother and his "sacrifice" welled up. Who are these men and women to offer themselves to our defense, willing to be sent off to God knows where to fight and die? For us? For themselves? For the ideas called America – freedom – democracy? Is it an immature rush to glory? What comparison to a guy like me whose life is marked by egotism, materialism, and self-preservation? Why would they pay such a price for some politician's whims, or religious beliefs, or greed? I haven't paid a price for anything I've got in this world, and yet these guys...why do they do it? The soldier looked over at Harold and smiled.

"Merry Christmas," Harold said, surprised at himself as he normally did not speak to strangers.

"Merry Christmas, sir," said the soldier, pausing by Harold's seat.

"Headed home" Harold couldn't help staring at the brightly colored rows of ribbons and silver emblems on the man's chest.

"Yes." Harold studied his neighbor closely. The man wore his gray hair with a close crew cut, had a neatly trimmed moustache, and had penetrating black eyes behind gold rimmed glasses. His was of average height, and the way he sat revealed a physical fitness Harold had not known since his teenage years.

"Christmas with your family?"

"My daughter and her husband. And three grandkids."

"You been service in a long time?"

"I'll have my thirty done next year. Retire."

"That rank on your sleeve. It's not familiar to me."

"Sergeant Major. Not many of us left." The bartender came over to the two men. She was a pretty woman in her mid-thirties. Shapely, wearing a white blouse, red jacket and black slacks.

"Sorry to keep you gents waiting. What'll it be?"

"You go ahead," the sergeant gestured to Harold.

"Can you make a martini?

"Vodka or gin?

"Gin. Dry, up, and with a lemon peel." The bartender nodded.

"I'll have an Irish Coffee, if that's possible," the sergeant major asked.

"Jaimeson's?" the bartender asked.

"Perfect. And some sugar on the side, please." The woman moved away to do her work.

"I guess you've been through a lot," Harold suggested.

"Seen my share. I was drafted at the tail end of Vietnam. I decided to stay in. We rebuilt the Army in the eighties...then was in the middle of all that high tech stuff that came in the nineties."

"I take it you've seen combat."

"Vietnam, Panama, Grenada, the Gulf, Afghanistan. I'm just back from Iraq a week."

"Wow. What are you going to do after you retire?"

"I really haven't thought that far yet." He grinned. "Truth is I'm not sure about retiring. I never thought I'd get this far." Harold's martini arrived. He didn't touch it, waiting for the sergeant's drink to appear.

"Can I ask you a question?"

"Fire away."

"Why did you do it?"

"Do what?"

"Spend your life as a soldier?"

"Well it didn't start out that way. Like I said, there was the draft back then when I was young. I figured I'd go in for my two years and some reserve time and get it behind me. A lot of people were joining the National Guard or getting deferments to stay out. My day wasn't rich. College wasn't me." He smiled and shook his head. "And, plain and simple, found out I liked it. Damn clear way of living. They got rules for everything, books, manuals, regulations. Didn't take a genius to find out what to do, how to do it, and when to do it. It al felt natural to me. So I took a re-up. Then another. Vietnam ended and we...I mean soldiers, weren't welcome by many folks. I stayed with my own, I guess. Time started to pass. Next thing I know, I'm a lifer. Life sure does pass quickly."

"I hear that," Harold said. He liked this guy. He liked his simple honesty and gentle manner. "But what about all that? I mean is it enough?" Harold pointed to the man's ribbons.

"Enough?"

"Accomplishments." The sergeant's Irish Coffee arrived. He thanked the bartender and stirred the whipped cream into the steaming brown liquid. Then he poured some sugar on top of that. He lifted his cup. "Merry Christmas," he said. They clinked drinks. Harold took a long sip, as did the soldier.

"These ribbons are all sort of my life as a visual. I'm proud to be a soldier. I'm proud to have fought for my country. It's a simple as that."

"But like you said, after Vietnam it was a bad time for soldiers"

"Yes. But times change. These days I can't pay for a cup of coffee or a drink in a public place, some stranger comes up and says it's on me." He held up his hand. "And don't try it here. This one's on me." Harold nodded. "What about yourself? Did you ever serve?"

"No. I work on Wall Street. But my brother-in-law was in. He uh...we lost him in the first Gulf War." The Sergeant Major nodded and sipped his coffee while Harold wondered why he had said that, and why he felt proud to have done so.

CHAPTER EIGHT

REMEMBRANCES

George's truck was in four-wheel drive as it moved along the county road. He'd had this Chevy for twelve years. One-hundred-forty-three thousand miles. It still had the   original transmission. Not too much rust on the rocker panels. He listened carefully to the low rumble of the engine. He trusted the vehicle, but like any machine he relied on, it needed attention from time to time. But it was running beautifully now, carrying him on a most important mission. Ahead, a yellow school bus, festooned with Christmas decorations, was stopped near a farmhouse. The snow picked up a little. It was going to be a solid storm. A girl, hauling a cumbersome tuba case, made her way down the driveway of the farmhouse toward the bus. George could see the bus was filled with kids from the New Chatham High School band. A few of the kids had opened their windows and were cheering their tuba player on. George reasoned that they were probably heading to the Chatham county retirement home where they always gave the residents there a concert on Christmas Eve. Once the girl was on board, the bus driver waved for George to go on ahead of him. As he pulled out, his oversized tires slipped momentarily, then grabbed the layer of sand under the fresh snow. The snowplows will be busy tonight, he thought. The drivers would miss quality time with their families. As he passed the bus several of the kids waved to him. He waved back to them, and for a moment, conjured up a mental image of John in their young, hopeful faces. Leaving the school bus behind, he moved back into the storm, unobstructed. The rate of snowfall increased so he clicked up the speed of the windshield wipers a notch and raised the heat level of the front window defroster. The image of John with the kids on the bus stayed with him, and then he was in his workshop with his son...

"No, Dad," John pronounced adamantly, "it's you who refuses to understand. It's my life. It's my decision. I'm over eighteen. I just want your approval." They stood close to one another in the center of George's workshop in the barn. The four neat workbenches, each with a project in the works, waited for attention...Jan Williamson's Bentwood rocker that needed a new cane seat; his tractor's

water pump waiting for new gaskets; kitchen cabinets for Laurie Sellick; and new shelving for an 18th century armoire the Phillips' had bought at an antique auction. A rack of overhead fluorescent lamps illuminated the area. The mingled aromas of George's work, sawdust, oil, and varnish, lingered in the air.

"I admire your motives, and your guts son, but I'm afraid...all the way down to my toes."

"Yeah, well I'm not."

"It's not your fear. It's mine!" George softened his tone. "Why can't you try college, Johnny? A few years is all I'm asking. You have so much potential. You know no one in our family has ever been to college and I..."

"I'll go when I finish my tour," John said, cutting his father off. "I promise." John picked up The New Chatham Sentinel and showed the front page to George. "Have you seen this, dad?" The article was titled "Local Boy Qualifies Airborne."

"No, I haven't." George took the paper and glanced at the article.

"Larry James went Airborne. He was on the baseball team with me last year. Left field. That's what I want to do. I'm just not interested in college... not now anyway."

"I'm saying give it a try first. The army will be always there. Maybe you could try for OCS – then be an officer after graduation. Maybe we could look at West Point. Mom's cousin Arthur is a Assemblyman downstate."

"That's not what I want to do. I've got to go now. You went... You should understand."

"Vietnam was different. In those days either you were in school, or married with kids, or had a well connected daddy...or you got drafted. I didn't have a choice. You do." John didn't want to hear this. He turned away. "What can I say to make you see how wrong this is?" George put his hands on John's shoulders. "We don't want you to go, son. We're your parents. We love you. We don't want anything to happen."

"It's done," John said with finality in his voice. "I went into Albany this morning and signed the Army enlistment papers. They say it's up to me to qualify Airborne after I go through Basic and AIT. I leave in two weeks." And that was that. It was done. George felt weak in his knees and heaviness in his chest. Then his heart fluttered and he was momentarily dizzy. He steadied himself against the workbench. His movement knocked a ripsaw blade onto the floor. The hollow tinny sound on the

hardwood floor echoed in the air like a tolling bell.

"So that's it?" George finally said. His voice was thin. Choked.

"That's it." George took a deep breath of resignation.

"All right. What's done is done," George said swallowing hard. "We'd better tell your mother." He put his arm around his son's broad shoulder, and turned out the light. When had his baby boy grown so tall and strong?

They stepped from the warm, brightly-lit workshop into the chill night air. A light snow dusted them as they walked toward the house. John's ardor to join conjured up visions of lean, young men, in their skivvies, waiting for a perfunctory physical before being transported to basic training bases. His memory zipped through the hot spring at Fort Dix, New Jersey; the mind numbing heat and humidity of summer Fort Jackson, South Carolina; his first dangling trip up the three hundred foot tower at Fort Benning, Georgia. And then, that indelible memory of walking alone, down the gangplank of the chartered airliner, in his khakis, at the big Tan Son Nhut air base. That memory melted to another - a jungle clearing with nine feet tall stalks of razor-

sharp elephant grass blowing wildly in the rotor downdraft. He was perched on the edge of a Huey, and, as the swaying helicopter closed onto the LZ he jumped out into the jungle clearing sprinting toward the tree line expecting an AK-47 round between the eyes. Behind and above him the door gunner fired his M60 into the jungle. Two Cobra Gun ships swooped past overhead, firing rockets as they simultaneously raked the verdant jungle with their deadly 7.62mm Mini-gun.

"And for Christ sake, don't ever, ever, volunteer for anything," George told John as they stopped at the back door of the house. "Keep in the middle, keep your head down, and don't let them know your name. Can you remember that?"

"I will, dad. I will."

They entered the house and paused in the mudroom. Carol was in the kitchen pouring some melted butter on a bowl of popcorn. When she saw the somber expression on George's face she knew something was wrong. George stood by helplessly as John told his mother he had joined the army.

"No!" was all she said. "No. No. No..." Over and over. She was shaking uncontrollably. When John tried to hold her, she spun away with such an

angry force that the bowl of popcorn spun out of her hands. The white, puffy, kernels exploded into the air and floated all over the kitchen floor like a burst of snow.

George was snapped out of his daydream as the popcorn became real snow pelting the windshield. His wipers were barely keeping up as the storm intensified. He clicked them up to the maximum and leaned forward, peering through the truck's nearly obliterated windshield. It was growing dark now. He slowed down and clicked on his high beams, but that only illuminated the heavy snowflakes and cut down his vision. He went back to normal beams. The wind was picking up too. He turned the defroster fan up to maximum too. The inside of cab was getting very warm. He mused that the old heater was working well – too well. He drove past the black, iron gates to the cemetery. Through the swirls of white that engulfed him now, another daydream floated up bearing visions that he had long kept sealed away in that part of his soul where painful memories reside...

First Lieutenant Gary Osborne stepped down from the passenger seat of the olive drab Army van, cocking his black beret at a slight angle before his highly shined low quarters touched the frozen earth. The contrast between the brilliant blue winter sky and the drab, lifeless earth was stark. Lieutenant Osborne was slightly more than six feet tall, with close cropped hair, and the tinge of tan from the Afghanistan sun remaining on his face. His tailored Class-A green uniform fit him well. Three rows of ribbons, including a Purple Heart and Silver Star, stood out above his left breast pocket. Atop them was a blue and silver Combat Infantryman's Badge. He paused for a moment to survey the slope of the hill down to the waiting grave, and then checked his watch as the door slid back on the van and Staff Sergeant Alexander Hunt stepped out into the cold winter sunlight. A green canopy stood near the gravesite. Metal folding chairs were set in rows under its shelter. A roll of artificial green turf covered the bare earth of the open grave and its surrounding banks. The wide, white straps of the lowering mechanism, strung across its chrome frame, awaited the arrival of Staff Sergeant John Boyajian's casket. As Lieutenant Osborne gazed at the neatly tended rows of gravestones in the small country cemetery, he heard the sound of the van door sliding back.

Staff Sergeant Hunt was a short, African-American man with penetrating eyes, and a powerful physique. The sergeant exemplified the long tradition of non-commissioned officers running the army. His was tough but fair. Above all he looked out for the interests of the soldiers under him. He was a born teacher and leader, exuding confidence and conviction which was quickly shared by his men. Sergeant Hunt snapped a salute to Lieutenant Osborne.

Lieutenant Osborne was the Officer in Charge, Sergeant Hunt was the Non-commissioned officer in charge, and with them were a pallbearer and firing party of six other soldiers, and a bugler. This was Lieutenant Osborne's third rendering of full military honors to an active duty soldier killed in action in two weeks. The first time he led a Burial Honors Detail at gravesite he felt rigid and ill at ease waiting for the deceased soldier's family to ask him why he had returned home alive and not the fallen soldier. He remembered the stories his uncle had told him about leading funeral details into Kentucky and Tennessee in 1969; of the reactions of those families ranging from gratitude for the military honors, to hatred of the Yankees bringing home yet another southern soldier. He had been intensely moved by the grief of the family, as were the other soldiers of the detail. He had focused intensely on each action, each command, each word he or his team were trained to do or say. By the second Burial Honors Detail he had been able to disengage ever so slightly from the grieving family. He knew he had to do that, and he had to get the other soldiers in his detail to be able to do that if they were to survive the anticipated dozen military funerals they were expected to conduct over the next month.

Lieutenant Osborne thought that, in many ways, burial duty was a lot like a combat operation. You planned, you trained, you knew someone wasn't coming back, but you couldn't think about it. You had to think about the mission. You couldn't let the grief dim the focus of your attention on completing the mission. Lieutenant Osborne, Staff Sergeant Hunt, and the enlisted men had been picked arbitrarily for this assignment, hurriedly trained and tested over the course of a few days, and then, just a day later, given their orders to provide Full Military Funeral Honors for the first time. They had all been shaken by the experience. Lieutenant Osborne remembered walking the halls of a motel on the outskirts of Amsterdam, New York, after the *first time his team had buried a fellow soldier. He went room to room, soldier to soldier, speaking with each man. They were all shaken by this aspect of the loss of a fellow soldiers; a ceremony they had not seen before. Buddies and strangers had died; some in their arms, many mutilated and suffering before death's graceful curtain. And now they were part of the final ceremony - present along with the mothers, fathers, grandparents, brothers, sisters, sweethearts...children. As in combat, each member of the detail had to find their own way in coping. After the funeral, each soldier found himself looking in a mirror containing a reflection of himself, and his fallen comrade, and again, could only wonder why he was still alive.*

"I'll get the team ready, sir," the sergeant said.

"We've got some time, Sergeant. Let's run through it one more time."

"Yes sir." Lieutenant Osborne returned the salute and watched Hunt lead his team of eight down the hill to the gravesite. Sunlight glinted off their highly polished black shoes. Their uniforms were smartly pressed and tailored. Sergeant Hunt directed the bugler to a concealed position nearby the grave. The young corporal trudged over the slope until he

was out of sight. 'Bertram's got a passion for that horn,' thought Lieutenant Osborne. 'Each time we do this his soul is in every note.' As Hunt put the squad through the ceremony, Obsorne saw some cars arrive and park inside the cemetery gates. He looked across the sea of headstones again.

"How many of you are out there," said Lieutenant Osborne softly into the wind. "World Wars, Korea, Vietnam, Somalia, Afghanistan, Iraq? How many of you found eternal peace in this place?" Lieutenant Osborne saw the funeral cortege approach. He signaled to Sergeant Hunt who held his men in position. They were ready. The hearse pulled to a stop at the base of the hill with the following limousines and cars stopping behind it. Six tall strapping young men, former members of the high school baseball team who played with John Boyajian, stepped to the rear of the hearse and gently slid the flag draped casket out. They paused, then lifted it and slowly, respectfully, John's friends carried the remains of their friend to his final resting place.

"Attention!" commanded Sergeant Hunt. The Burial Honors Detail stood rigidly correct with eyes forward. "Present arms!" The young soldiers saluted. As the coffin approached the gravesite,

Lieutenant Osborne moved to a spot overlooking the gravesite where he could see both Sergeant Hunt, and the bugler. The pallbearers placed the coffin containing John Boyajian's remains on the lowering device.

"Order arms!" said Sergeant Hunt. He then stepped with precision to the head of the casket, as a young buck sergeant stepped to the foot. In one motion, inseparable by their individual actions, the two soldiers made a minute adjustment to ensure the flag was level, stretched out, and centered over John's coffin. Just as smartly, they stepped back, turned, and marched to rejoin the other members of the team.

Lieutenant Osborne watched the family and friends of another dead soldier approach another grave. Mourners gathered around the flag draped coffin. The Lieutenant recognized George, Carol, and Jennifer Boyajian from his visit to the funeral home to discuss the graveside ceremony and, though it was not part of the mandated Full Military Funeral Honors, Lieutenant Osborne had begun placing an American flag to the rear of the coffins of his fallen fellow soldiers at the funeral parlor, and then had each member of the Burial Honors Detail slowly and with great reverence march silently toward the coffin, halt, and snap a salute of respect and honor to the fallen, and to the flag. The raw emotional power of the gesture from one soldier to another had moved his men, and he knew it touched the families. In one small way, it was a sign of respect, of love, and of comradeship demonstrated by those who had served as had the fallen.

The family and friends of joined George and Carol Boyajian, and Jennifer, as they all gathered silently at graveside. Larry and Jan Williamson, Mary Simpson and her daughter Sara; Elizabeth and her parents, Tom and Sylvia Jennings, and dozens of John's classmates from high school. Two of the former high school athletes helped Larry Williamson negotiate the track from the asphalt road across the lawn to the grave site in his wheel chair.

Lieutenant Osborne had been raised in a small town in Georgia. He knew how close knit families and friends became over the generations. He could see how much Staff Sergeant Boyajian had been a part of this town. For an instant he thought of his own funeral and wondered who might attend.

As many as could sat on the cold metal folding

chairs under the green canopy. The rest spilled out on all sides, surrounding the family in a circle of love. Lieutenant Osborne could not hear the words but he knew what they might be as the minister opened his Bible to a selected passage; surely one of meaning to the parents and Sergeant Boyajian. After about fifteen minutes noticed the minister looked up at Mister Boyajian, and then toward Sergeant Hunt. Osborne knew the committal service was nearing an end. He traced the path he would take for his role in the ceremony. The reverend then nodded to Sergeant Hunt who stepped to the head of the casket.

"Present arms!" Sergeant Hunt and the other members of the team snapped to attention and saluted.

The first crack of the M16's firing ripped the air and rattled the sky. 'Well done,' Osborne thought. 'All as one.' The gunfire caused some of the mourners to jump or flinch. Some reached out for those near them to steady themselves. George Boyajian held his sobbing wife tight to his chest. Tears streamed down George's face. Young Jennifer clutched her father from the other side and buried her face in his coat. 'The first volley always gets them,' Osborne thought. They see the raised rifles, and they know it's coming, but knowing and feeling are two verey different things...' The second crack slammed home the finality of John's death; it conjured nightmarish images of the battlefield on which he died in the minds of some.   'Tears with the second one,' Osborne's conscience told him.

The third crack took George Boyajian back to his own war and consumed him with the pain of his son's death.   'Grief...open unabashed grief with the third,' was the Lieutenant's final observation.   He signaled to the bugler.   The diminutive red-haired corporal played "Taps" with feeling and sincerity for the fallen; the family; the nation.   After the last, dying, trembling note echoed across the cemetery, Osborne snapped a quick salute of well done to the bugler; a one on one mark of respect from one soldier to another; and then marched as proudly as he could muster toward the grave.   Sergeant Hunt and the younger buck sergeant snapped to attention, both now standing at opposite end of the casket. With rigid deliberation they pulled the flag taut and raised it above the casket, then took three side steps away from it and the mourners.   With precise and distinct movements Sergeant Hunt folded the flag in triangular folds, one upon the other until only seven silver stars against a deep blue background were showing.   The mourners watched the ceremony in muted respect. Neatly, Hunt tucked the edge of the flag into the pocket made by the last fold, then did an exact about face to where his Lieutenant now stood. Osborne saluted the flag resting on the palms of Sergeant Hunt's hands, and then lowered his arm. With profound dignity, Lieutenant Osborne extended his hands palms up toward Sergeant Hunt. The sergeant placed the flag on the lieutenant's hands, stepped back smartly, and saluted. Lieutenant Osborne took a deep breath and walked slowly and deliberately to George Boyajian while Sergeant Hunt took his place at the head of the soldiers near the casket and led them smartly away from the gravesite toward the firing squad. The firing squad, waiting at attention, joined the tail of Sergeant Hunt's column as it passed. Together, they marched up the hill toward to their van.

Lieutenant Osborne watched George Boyajian stiffen in his seat. He helped his sobbing wife to sit more erect in her chair as he gestured toward the approaching officer and flag. Carol shook her head and tried to look away from the approaching flag. Lieutenant Osborne understood her reaction all too well. If somehow Mrs. Boyajian could refuse to accept the flag, then perhaps none of this was real. She would awake from a horrible dream and her son, John, would be on his way home for the rest of his life. Osborne was the messenger that denied that dream forever.

He stood at attention in front of George Boyajian. Both men looked into each other's eyes. George tilted his head slightly toward his wife. Lieutenant Osborne knew the words he was directed to say, but he knew he wouldn't say those words exactly as written... 'This flag is presented on behalf of a grateful nation and the United States Army as a token of appreciation for your loved one's honorable and faithful service.' "How can I present this as a "token" on this day?" he worried. Carol was mesmerized by the sight of the young officer before her. She caught the sunlight glinting from his Combat Infantryman's Badge, and the metal devices fixed to his ribbons. She did not know what they meant specifically other than that this young man standing before her was a soldier who served his country and had come to honor her fallen son.
Lieutenant Osborne bent forward and offered the flag to Carol Boyajian. He could see the despair in her eyes as she accepted the flag.

"This flag," said Lieutenant Osborne with measured diction, "is presented on behalf of a grateful nation and the United States Army, in

abiding respect, for Staff Sergeant John Boyajian's honorable and faithful service, and sacrifice." He then stepped back, saluted, turned and marched alone up the hill to the waiting van. Behind him he heard the plaintive wail of a mother lamenting the death of her child. Chills coursed down his spine. Tears welled up in his eyes. Fifty yards...he only had to make fifty yards to the van. He fought to compose himself.

"Lieutenant! Lieutenant! Wait!" Osborne turned to see George Boyajian walking quickly toward him. He stood at attention and braced himself not knowing what to expect. Would it be hatred and anger that his son came home in a box? Would it be inconsolable grief, or red hot rage? He owed this father his moment whatever it brought. As George neared Osborne could see the older man's breath was coming hard he climbed the slope. As he neared the Lieutenant took note of tears flooding this father's eyes. He stopped close by.

"Lieutenant," said George catching his breath. "I wanted to thank you," cried the father, nodding toward the gravesite, "for what you," he sobbed, "and your men did. For what you said. Thank you for honoring my son." George wiped his tears with his sleeves. "This has got to be tough duty."

"Yes sir. It surely is."

"How many?" asked George.

"This is my third, sir."

"Doesn't get any easier, does it?"

"I pray to God sir that it never does."

CHAPTER NINE

AN INVITATION

George's reminiscence suddenly disappeared when something moving on the road ahead caught his eye. He slammed his foot down on the brake pedal. The old Chevy's brakes locked. He went into a skid. He struggled at the wheel, pumping, then easing off on the pedal, until he gained some control. Then the pickup spun again and skidded to a stop. The rear tires had slid down into a small drainage ditch on the side of the road. Fortunately he had not been traveling fast. George gathered himself and shut off the engine, but left his lights and flasher on. Of all the rotten luck, this had to happen now. Darned daydreaming. He made a mental note to be more aware, then opened the door and jumped down into the deepening snow. The wind gusted and swirled around him. He trudged around his truck, inspecting for damage, but saw none.

"Now," he pondered aloud, "how do I get out of this ditch? And what the hell was that I saw on the road?" He stepped up from the ditch, out of the protection of the truck's body. A gust of snowy wind momentarily blinded him. He steadied himself against the pickup and brushed the thick flakes away from his eyes. Seemingly from nowhere, a man appeared in front of him. 'So that's what I saw before I swerved', George thought. The man slapped his palms against his arms to keep warm. In the truck's lights George saw the man had no gloves. He wore old, army-style jump boots, faded blue denims, and a brown leather bomber jacket zipped tightly up to his neck, its fur collar up. A black navy watch cap covered his head and ears. At his feet, a battered canvas Army B-4 bag lay in the accumulating snow. The man appeared to be in his mid-thirties, but in this weather and dim light, it was hard to actually tell. George looked up and down the deserted road, now obliterated by snow. "Sweet Jesus!" George exclaimed. "Where in the hell did you come from? I didn't see... Uh... Are you okay?"

"I'm fine," the man answered, smiling and extending his hand. "Name's Matthew." George shook his hand – glove to bare skin. Oddly, George felt the warmth of the stranger's hand through his glove.

"I'm George... George Boyajian. I'm really sorry. I...I didn't see...The snow picked up suddenly..."

"Hey George. It's no problem. You missed me."

Matthew smiled and glanced at the truck. "But we'd better get you out of there and turned around before anyone else comes along." He picked up his B-4 bag. George got into the truck, started the engine, and revved it. He began to rock the truck back and forth while Matthew pushed against the tailgate in synch with the rocking. While they struggled to free the pickup from the ditch the storm grew stronger until there was a near whiteout. Finally, as George hammered the accelerator, Matthew gave one powerful, grunting, heave and the truck broke free and slid up onto the road.

"Ta-da!" Matthew sang out, waving his arms theatrically like a magician's flourish at the end of a trick.

"Hop in," George yelled out the window. The stranger settled into the wide passenger seat. He chucked his bag behind, in the storage bay.

"I haven't seen a bag like that for quite a while," George remarked as they began to drive. That's issue, isn't it?"

"I did my time," Matthew answered. George concentrated on being cautious as he drove down the snow covered road.

"See any action?" Matthew looked through the

windshield as the truck's headlights illuminated a snow covered field beyond a curve ahead. George glanced over at Matthew. He recognized the 'thousand yard stare' - to a place and time far away.

"Yeah, I did. The Gulf... Desert Storm."

"Special Forces?"

"Right. The 5th," Matthew said, "How'd you know that?" A rush pulsed through George. 'The 5th!'

"You guys have a certain look...a way about you."

"What about you?"

"Vietnam. 101st." Matthew nodded.

"So when were you there?" George asked. He was not just making conversation. He was curious. The 5th SF was John's unit.

"From the get-go - arrived in October '90. We were Desert Shield getting ready for Desert Storm. Headed up into Indian Country before the legs arrived."

"Legs," said George smiling. "Haven't heard that expression in a long time. Airborne...Most men can't take a ten foot jump from a step ladder. Why did you want to jump out of perfectly good airplanes?"

"If I was going to do it, I wanted to be the best,"

Matthew said softly, but with the confidence of a man who has done it.

"Most people your age don't serve." Matthew smiled. "Most people never find their compass. I guess you and I did George. We must have been about the same age when we went in."

"You get hit?"

"I carry some scars...some memories that won't fade."

"Was it worth it?"

"To my way of thinking, this would be one meaningless life without a little danger and sacrifice." George liked this man.

"What about the politics...the people? Like now. Afghanistan was acceptable, but half the country doesn't believe we ought be fighting in Iraq."

"Politics has got nothing to do with the honor in soldiering. That's what drew me. Either you're going to be a worm in the earth, blind and insulated, or you going to soar." Matthew laughed. "I chose to soar by..." George joined Matthew in the old saw...

"...jumping out of perfectly good airplanes."

George wanted to pursue more, but he suppressed the impulse. Matthew was a stranger. John had been on his mind all day. Too much daydreaming. The snow and the road needed his attention. There was moment of silence in rhythm to the wipers beating off the snow.

"So," George finally said, "I guess you're headed toward town?" Matthew leaned his head back against the seat.

"Actually, I was on my way to Route 22... Tryin' to get to the Interstate. I'm going to hook up with my ride there in the morning. I guess being Christmas and all, folks are charitable. I've been makin' real good time and I'm way ahead of schedule."

"The morning you say? What're you going to do 'till then?" Matthew rubbed his hands together in front of the heater vent.

"Man. That feels good. Flop somewhere, I guess."

"There's a Day's Inn the other side of town. Nothin' fancy, but it's clean and close to the Interstate. I can drop you there."

"Sounds good but, well, I'm a little short right now. Maybe there's a bus station where I could crash?" George glanced at Matthew suspiciously.

"Goin' home to spend Christmas with your family?" Matthew stared out the window. They were now on the outskirts of town. Here the snow at the edge of the road was muddy brown from the plows, sand and salt. The storm's intensity had eased.

"No. I don't really have a family, George. Did once... Not anymore."

"Not in any uh... trouble, are you?" George asked with a frown.

"You mean like with the law?"

"Like that I guess..."

"No sir. I always follow the rules." His tone and attitude satisfied George who then reached across the cab and gently tapped Matthew on the knee.

"Good! Now listen to me. No motel and no bus station for you. Tonight you have a family. You're gonna spend Christmas Eve with us!" Matthew sat up.

"No. I couldn't do that. I mean what's your family going to think? Bringing a stranger home... especially on Christmas Eve?"

"Not to worry. You'll be welcome. If a man doesn't have room for another on Christmas Eve, then when does he, huh?" Matthew nodded.

"Well...thank you George," Matthew said. He leaned back again, against the worn fabric of his seat, and relaxed.

"There's uh, one thing I guess you should know about us," George said softly. "We haven't celebrated Christmas for a long time. A very long time."

CHAPTER TEN

STARS AND ANGELS

Jennifer sat on the couch in the living room observing David as he carefully separated various ornaments into groups. Animals, Santa's, angels, balls, cones, and all the handmade ones they made or were given to the family over the years. Some were very old, carried more than one hundred years ago by a distant great-grandmother of George's from Armenia to a new home in America. Jennifer sipped her cold coffee then dunked her last Oreo cookie in it, savoring the sweet mixture of soft, wet chocolate and icing.

"Success!" Carol announced as she entered the living room carrying an old brown shopping bag. "I knew it had to be up there somewhere."

"How on earth did you remember?"

"Your mother's a pack-rat. Never throw anything out. Now, let's see." Hesitantly, Carol reached down into the bag and removed an object wrapped in tissue paper. She carefully unwrapped what was once an electric five-pointed star, only one of its points was broken off, and missing. "Oh my Jenny. Remember this?" Jennifer instantly recognized the star. Carol handed it to her and went back to exploring the bag's contents. Jennifer clutched the star to her breast and closed her eyes...

A teenage John was with her in this very living room. She was five years old. It was late afternoon – Christmas Eve. Lights and ornaments surrounded them. Dad was at work. Mom was in the kitchen preparing dinner. They were given the task of starting to decorate the tree.

"Oh! This one Johnny. Let's put this one on first." She grasped the pretty five-pointed star with its electric cord trailing behind. Young Jennifer was filled with a child's excitement of Christmas to come.

"Okay little sister. Where do you want it?" She frowned at the 'little' reference.

"On the top, silly. Where else would the star go? And I'm not little."

"Right you are," he said. He looked around the cluttered living room. "But we'll need the ladder."

"No," she told him. "Just boost me up." She spread her arms out above her head.

"All-right! Here you go." John made a stirrup

by clasping his hands together. Jennifer, holding the star in one hand, stepped up onto John's hands.

"Are you strong enough?" she teased him.

"I don't know. You're right about not being little. You're getting pretty heavy." Jennifer giggled. With one foot in John's clasped hands she leaned one hand on his shoulder and reached with the other to place the star on top of the tree.

"Can you make it?" John asked. Jennifer stretched to

reach the top of the tree.

"Almost... Just a little more... Uh-oh!" She lost her balance causing her weight to suddenly shift. John staggered back, trying to keep his balance and not drop his sister. He backed across the living room until he struck the arm of the sofa, then continued backward onto the sofa, bringing a screaming and laughing Jennifer down on top of him. They both lay there for a moment, laughing together. Jennifer looked at the star and noticed that one of the points had broken off.

"I guess it won't be as bright." Jennifer giggled.

"No matter," he told her. "It will still always shine for us."

The daydream passed, and Jennifer opened her eyes.

She was still clutching the now four-pointed star.

"I feel so cheated that he didn't come home. He was a good brother. He was my friend." Carol was surprised at Jenny's reminiscence, but noticed her clutching the star and understood.

"Are you talking about Uncle John?" David asked.

"Yes, darling," Jennifer answered. "I just remembered how much I miss him."

"Me too," David announced in a serious voice. Jennifer smiled at her son, glad to know he was sensitive, and comfortable enough to express it.

"I guess we're going to rake up some painful memories tonight," Carol said.

"Some good ones too," Jennifer added looking down at the star. Then she glanced back at David, again absorbed in his sorting. "And some new ones as well."

Later, when they had finished stringing out the new Christmas tree lights that George had purchased, and untangled the old ones, the three stepped back carefully. Several strings of lights now crisscrossed the living room floor, draped over the sofa, and threaded their way over the matching wing chairs on either side of the fireplace.

"That's it," Carol stated.

"It looks like spaghetti, Grandma," David announced. They all laughed.

"I guess it does. Do you remember what you used to call spaghetti?"

"When I was a baby? Yes... pishghetti."

"That's right. It always made Grandpa laugh." Then Carol picked up the plug that led to the extension cord where all the lights were connected. "Okay. Here goes." She inserted it into the wall socket near the window. All the lights came on, brilliant and full, casting a kaleidoscopic glow of red, green, blue, yellow and white across the room.

"Wow," said David."

"I'd forgotten," Jennifer said softly.

"Mmmmmmmm," was all that Carol could muster. Her heart skipped a beat, and she shuddered. "They'll look wonderful on the tree, won't they?" she finally said. Before Jenny could answer the sound of a car door slamming outside broke the spell the lights had cast.

"Grandpa!" David shouted. "The tree is here!"

"I'll go give him a hand," Jennifer said as she headed for the front door closet to get a jacket.

"Be careful dear," Carol called after her. "The snow is deep. Maybe you should put on boots."

Jennifer was slipping on her jacket when there was a knock. She opened the front door to find Mary Simpson standing there with a tin of cookies in her hand.

"Oh... It's you Mrs. Simpson."

"Hello Jenny. How are you dear heart?"

"Fine...I'm just fine. Oh. Sorry. Come in." Mary stepped into the foyer. Carol and David stood there, expecting George. Silent disappointment registered on David's face.

"Mary!" Carol exclaimed. "What a surprise." The two women hugged. "How nice to see you."

"It's been a while," Mary said. "Thanksgiving I believe." She handed the tin of cookies to Carol. "I baked them fresh this morning. When I heard Jenny was home I just had to come by. I believe they're her favorites – chocolate chip. And there's some butternut for you Carol. Merry Christmas."

"Why thank you. How sweet. That pie Thanksgiving was luscious." She opened the tin and showed the cookies to David. "How about this David? You know Mrs. Simpson is the best baker in town." The boy eyed the cookies. Chocolate chip and butter nut. He decided Mrs. Simpson was okay.

"They look good, Grandma." Carol gave them to David to hold.

"Mary, this is my grandson David." Mary Simpson extended her hand to David. He took it for a quick shake.

"I saw you once when you were a little baby. You've grown up nicely, David." David held the cookies. Their sweet aroma made his stomach grumble.

"How about a cup of coffee? I've got some on." Carol offered.

"Tea would be nice. But just for a minute. I'd love to stay longer dear, but I can't. I'm on my way to church. The choir. You know..."

"Of course. Christmas Eve." Carol went into the kitchen. Mary rolled her eyes to Jennifer.

"Pastor Raymond has us doing a section from Handel's Messiah. Can you imagine?"

"I bet it'll sound great," Jennifer said as they followed Carol into the kitchen. David followed, munching on a cookie. When they got to the kitchen Carol had water up to boil.

"Why don't you all come and see us tonight?" Mary asked. Both women were caught off guard by the invitation.

"Well, Mary... We uh... George is out right now. I don't know when he'll be back. But if he gets home in time, we will certainly...uh...try."

"Good. I'll look for you." The kettle whistled, announcing it was tea time. Jennifer and Mary sat at the table while Carol prepared the tea. "How about sharing some of those cookies with your mom and grandma?" Mary asked David. The boy brought them to the table and helped himself to another chocolate chip. Mary leaned close to Jennifer. "So...any new men in your life?" Jennifer was taken aback for a moment, but then realized it was typically something Mary would say. She was not known to be shy or retiring.

"No. Nobody at the moment..." Mary nodded.

"I see. Well, you're a pretty girl with your whole life ahead of you. You'll be just fine. Plenty of fish in the sea, Jenny. That's what I did since Ross died. Keeps the men on their toes..." Carol brought the tea to the table and sat down. David took another cookie and went to the window to watch the snow.

"Here we are," Carol said. Mary took a long sip of tea from her mug.

"Mmmmm. Nice. I was telling Jenny here to play the field."

"Yes... Well it's hard being a single mom and all..."

"I understand," Mary said. She took Jennifer's hand in hers. "One foot in front of the other...One day at a time." She patted Jennifer's hand and looked at Carol. "She'll be fine."

"I guess the whole town knows..." Jennifer said.

"The whole town loves you," Mary said. She got up. "And Pastor Raymond will hate me if I don't get to rehearsal." Carol and Jennifer got up. "You know, Carol, we miss your beautiful soprano voice. You're always welcome back..."

"Thank you, Mary," Carol said, slightly embarrassed. Mary then threw her arms around Jennifer and hugged her.

"You're going to have a healthy and happy New Year, Jenny. And many, many more. I feel it in my bones. You just have to feel it in your heart. Have faith."

"Thank you," Jennifer said, obviously touched. Mary turned to Carol and took her hands in hers. "You too, my dear. And if you can't make it later, Merry Christmas and a happy, healthy, New Year." She then went t the window where David stood. "Now you take care of your mother, David. I hope Santa is good to you tomorrow." She headed for the door – a whirlwind on the move. "Give George my best. He is a fine man Carol. You're so lucky to have him." She hugged Carol as an old friend would.

"Yes he is. Thank you, Mary. Merry Christmas." As Mary tucked her muffler beneath her coat collar, Carol realized that it was the first time in twelve years she had wished anyone a Merry Christmas.

"Now... Back out into that very white Christmas," Mary announced in a stoic but humorous way."

"How's the driving?" Jennifer asked.

"They're plowing. It's fine. God bless four-wheel drive." As she walked to the front door, Carol, Jennifer and David followed as if being pulled by her draft. They watched Mary go out into the dark, snowy night.

"She's so...so enthusiastic," Carol said as they watched Mary trudge through the snow to her Bronco. David had another cookie and was munching on it. "But sweet, and a good friend."

"I guess everyone knows I'm dying," Jennifer said dreamily.

"They don't, and you're not!"

"Right, Mom." She yawned. "Anyway, I'm a little tired. I think I'll go upstairs."

"What about trimming the tree? There's still a lot to do before dad gets here."

"You and David get started. I'll pitch in later." Carol watched Jennifer walk slowly up the stairs, and then went into living room with David. She glanced out the window, hoping to see George coming down the driveway. The storm had let up considerably. But all she saw was Mary's taillights as she turned onto the road at the end of their driveway. And then it was dark. No sign of George. David was finishing his cookie.

"Okay David. It looks like it's up to you and me to get ready for the tree. That's enough cookies for you." She took the tin from him. "I'll put these in the kitchen and look after dinner for a bit. Why don't you take those angels out of the box and start to place them around the room?"

"Okay, Grandma. Can I put one next to Uncle John's picture?"

"Yes dear. That's absolutely where an angel should go." As David went about the task with great care and ceremony, Carol went into the kitchen. She stopped by the window and looked out again at what appeared to be the last of the snowfall. Her mind drifted to another winter outside this window...

It was a bright day. Fifteen year old John was running and pulling his young sister along on an old but serviceable Flexible-Flyer in the plowed driveway. As they slid past the curve Jennifer spilled out into a snow bank. She laughed and rolled over on her back. John stopped to pick her up, but Jennifer began to move her arms and legs. She was making a "snow angel." John lay down next to her and made his own "snow angel." Afterward, they got up and admired their handiwork. Then Jenny hopped back on the sled and bade her 'horsy' to keep pulling. As they moved away on the sled, the image faded. The night returned.

Carol peered out at the snow, straining to see those two snow angels. But of course they were no longer there. Then she turned away from the window and began to think about diner.

CHAPTER ELEVEN

A TREE

By the time George and Matthew reached the outskirts of New Chatham the snow had let up. Though bright Christmas lights and decorations were everywhere, the streets were fairly deserted as the townspeople prepared for the holiday. They approached a gas station, and George pulled in.

"Lester is open. I need some gas. And I want to have a look at this old truck in the light." They stopped next to the gas pump. As George and Matthew got out, Lester Bukovsky came out of the office.

"Hey there George. What's up?"

"Fill 'er up, Les, will you?" George walked around the truck with Matthew.

"I may have screwed up the suspension," George said.

"The body looks okay to me." George knelt down and peered under at the axel of the rear right wheel."

"Something wrong?" Lester called out.

"I took a spin and ran it off into a ditch," George answered as he walked around to check the other front wheel and axel.

"How many miles do you have on it?" Matthew asked.

"One-thirty-nine."

"I guess she's a keeper," Matthew said with a smile.

"You want me to put her up on the rack?" Lester asked as he finished pumping the gas.

"No. Not tonight. What do I owe you?"

"Twenty-one eighty. But I've closed out the register. You just caught me in time."

"Put it on my tab."

"What tab?"

"Let me get this," Matthew offered. George put up his hand.

"No. That's okay. I'll straighten out with him later. Take it easy Les. Merry Christmas."

"You too, George. Have a good one." As the truck pulled away and Lester turned out the station lights he realized that was the first time in many years that George has wished him Merry Christmas. And then he wondered who the stranger was and why George had not introduced him.

"The tree farm is next to the church," George told Matthew as they got back onto the road. It shouldn't take too long."

"Not too many left, I imagine," Matthew said as he looked out the window. "This sure is a nice town."

"And growing. We've got lots of city people renovating and building weekend getaways. So, where are you from, Matthew?"

"No place in particular. I move around."

"What line of work you in?"

"Nothing steady. Sort of a Jack-of-all-trades and, as they say, master of none." He smiled. "How about you, George?"

"I'm a carpenter. Mostly home construction... Like I said, we have a lot of fixer-uppers happening now. And I do a little custom cabinet work. It's a busy time."

"Jesus was a carpenter," Matthew said.

"That's right. He surely was." Matthew reached for the radio knob. "How about some music?"

"Sure, John. See if you can find some carols."

"John?"

"Did I say John? I'm sorry. John was my son's name...He uh...he was killed in action."

"I'm sorry."

"Thanks. It was actually in Iraq... Desert Shield, that is." George took a deep breath. "He was Special Forces too. Like you. The 5ᵗʰ SFG. It was..." George couldn't finish the thought.

"I know... What I mean is, I hear you. We lost a few guys early on. But you didn't hear much of it. Black ops. I lost good friends there myself."

"Yeah, we ran a few black ops ourselves – went across a fence a couple of times. Hey...I'm glad you made it home." Matthew turned the knob on the radio, and tuned past several stations, pausing to listen. A frantic huckster...

"You got it, neighbors, Discount Dooley's of Albany's Pre-Christmas Christmas sale. Last night to take advantage of the big savings. So, come on down. Don't miss this once in a life..." Matthew turned the knob.

"It seems all holidays have become are reasons to shop," George said with disgust. A clipped male voice with a slight drawl came on as Matthew found another station.

"Yes, m'dear friends, it was over two thousand years ago, on this very night, that our Savior came into the world. We want to continue to bring you His message... His glad tidings... His peace and joy... So to do your part, for Jesus, right now... send your check or money order to...." Matthew turned the knob again. A choir singing 'We Three Kings' came on.

"Ahhh... Now that sounds like Christmas," George exclaimed. "John and I liked that one specially." He began to sing along with the radio. Matthew joined in. Their singing grew steadily louder. Unrehearsed, they blended into a pleasing harmony. George reached over and turned the radio volume up, then waved his arm as though leading a choir, and sang out in his basso profundo voice.

"Oh, star of wonder, star of night, star of royal beauty bright..." The two continued the duet as they drove around the square. They passed the hardware store just as Larry Williamson was locking up. He saw George's pickup approaching and then heard the two men singing as they passed by. He turned his wheelchair to watch as they passed by.

"Now there's something," he mused. "First Christmas lights, and now old George singing like the old days." Larry waved, but George was preoccupied with keeping the harmony and leading the chorale of two.

A few minutes later George eased to the curb next to the church - a three story Gothic stone structure.

Golden hued light escaped from its windows causing deep shadows to form within its parapets. It spilled onto the parking lot where the snow covered cars of the choir members sat. Strains of Handel's Messiah floated on the air. A string of white and yellow lights marked the boundary of the empty lot next door that was set up as a Christmas Tree park. Thick poles, with wire strung along them, and lights above, had held a beautiful crop of Christmas trees and wreaths for the past four weeks. But now, on the eve of Christmas, the pickings were sparse. The park seemed deserted. George and Matthew walked down the lanes between the few sad remaining trees and wreaths.

"Not much here," George said. "Nothing really full. That's the kind we always used to get." He glanced around the lot. "I wonder where Artie is. He's been selling trees here forever. Artie!" George called out. "Artie?"

There was no response. "Lights are on. He should be here somewhere. Artie! Maybe he's gone into the church for a nature call. Let's give it a minute or two. He's the only game in town, and if he's not around we may have to drive into Chatham, or Albany." Matthew went to the next aisle to look at a tree, but when he turned it was uneven and sparse.

George watched him as he walked back toward him. He decided to take a chance.

"Listen uh, Matthew... I know it sounds strange but, well, do you think you might have run into my son over there?" Matthew thought for a moment.

"Could be. John Boya...?"

"Boyajian. It's Armenian."

"I knew a lot of guys...casually. You see the job we did... Well, we stayed pretty much to ourselves."

"I see," George was disappointed. "Like life I guess," he said quietly. He looked around again for Artie.

"A philosopher, huh?"

"I had to be. You know. When John was gone I had a hole in me the size of the Grand Canyon. Booze and the Church didn't get it done. I had to find some rationale or go nuts."

"You mean peace of mind, or answers?"

"I gave up on answers."

"I hear that. But... Hey, this is the season of Peace. Maybe you'll find yours."

"I'm tryin' Matthew... I'm tryin'." Light snow began to fall again. A gust of wind caused the lights above the few remaining trees to sway and flicker. Then the sound of a deep, ugly, growl came from behind a small tent at the rear of the lot. Without warning, a large, agitated black German Shepherd appeared. Its eyes locked on George and Matthew as it inched toward them.

"Oh, man," George said backing away. "I forgot about that damned mutt." The dog, with fangs bared, came closer. He stopped ten short feet from Matthew. Matthew was still, but not afraid. At the same time, Artie, a wiry old man close to eighty, came out of the tent. He wore laced up hunting boots with brown flannel pants tucked into them. A threadbare, but serviceable navy P-coat and black watch cap completed his outfit. He wore no gloves over his gnarled, liver spotted, hands. A cloud of condensation streamed out of his mouth which was obliterated by a thick, tobacco stained, droopy moustache.

"Now you two be careful there," Artie called out. "He broke his darn chain again." Matthew dropped to one knee, fixing his stared at the dog.

"That's all right, boy. Take it easy." His voice was calm and assuring. The dog stopped growling. Artie came up next to George. Both men watched as the dog cautiously approached the kneeling Matthew. "Atta boy. I won't hurt you. C'mon Sport. C'mon," Matthew said softly. The dog was in front of Matthew. "That's a good boy, Sport. Yes."

The dog then sniffed Matthew's hand and licked his face. "You're a good boy, aren't you?" He petted the dog's head, and scratched his chest.

"You sure got a way with dogs, son. I never seen old Rex take to anyone so fast," Artie said with admiration in his voice.

"I love dogs," Matthew said, rising to his feet.

"Why did you call him Sport?" George asked.

"I don't know. It's just a name I call dogs. You know...like Rover or Buster."

"Sport was the name of John's dog," George said softly. A gust of wind snapped at his mackinaw. He shuddered, then clutched the neck of his jacket closed. "This all you have left, Artie?"

"You look at the date or time lately, George? I hear tell Santa's due in just a couple of hours." Artie's sarcasm was legendary around town. He was everyone's candidate for 'The most unforgettable character I ever met'. George couldn't help but smile.

"Yeah. One of his elves told me," he answered. "I guess I'm a little late."

"A little? Georgie old pal, you ain't bought a tree from me for what? Twelve or thirteen years?"

"I haven't bought from anyone. You know, Artie we..."

"Yeah, yeah" he said sadly. "I know." He touched George's shoulder. "You might have called. I'd have set one aside. I remember how you and the Misses always bought my fullest tree. Well, let's have a look see what's still around here." While George and Artie walked down the tree display, Rex pulled Matthew by the coat sleeve. He led the stranger to the far side of the tent where Matthew discovered a large full tree leaning against it.

"Hey George," Matthew called out. "Take a look over here." George came around the tent and saw the tree. It was dimly lit and draped in a light coating of snow, like it was still in the forest. Artie followed reluctantly, muttering something inaudible under his breath.

"That's it! That's the one! Great!" George took out his wallet. "How much, Artie?" Artie thrust his hands into his pockets, looked down, around the park, then at the church, and finally up into the now clearing night sky.

"You coulda called..."

"I'm sorry. Things uh... sometimes things change quickly. You know... At the last minute. So how much?" Artie gazed wistfully at the tree, and then at Matthew. The stranger smiled and arched his eyebrow in a questioning manner.

"Aw hell. It's getting' late," Artie muttered. "Probably won't have any more customers. I get stuck with these trees, I have to cart them off, you know?"

"So how much?" George wanted the tree badly.

"I'm an old man. Can't lug things around like I used to. Tell you what, George," Artie said in his best horse-trading manner. "You take this tree off my hands for ten bucks."

"Ten bucks? Are you nuts?"

"No Georgie, I ain't nuts. I'm a businessman. So next year you gotta buy the biggest I have...and I mean the biggest and at top dollar."

"Okay."

"And, you gotta do it the first day I open. No if's, and's or but's about it. You hear? So do we got a deal?" George slipped a ten dollar bill into Artie's outstretched palm.

"You bet! Deal." Not missing a beat, Artie turned and walked back to the tent. Rex followed. "Merry Christmas to you and the Misses," Artie said as he waved over his shoulder. "And say I said so to that pretty little daughter of yours." He closed the main flap of the tent.

"Merry Christmas, Artie," George called after him. Then he slapped Matthew on the shoulder.

"You're a lucky charm, Matthew." Both men lifted the tree and carried it to the pickup.

As they drove away Artie closed the cash box and switched off the lights. Rex sat patiently at his feet.

"Okay you old hairy mutt... Now you'll have to explain to mother why we gave our tree away." It seemed like Rex just smiled back at him. "Turncoat," Artie muttered as he lovingly rubbed the dog's ears.

Out on the road, George was as pleased as a child who just caught the biggest fish of his life. He was bubbling with joy.

"That, my new friend, is one great tree!"

"It sure is. Lucky it was still there."

"Yeah," George said, wondering for a fleeting moment himself how it had been missed by others. "Next year I'll do right by old Artie. One for our house, and one for the County Retirement Home. Yes sir. This Christmas is off to one great start."

"And you're sure about bringing me home?" Matthew asked. "I don't want to be a..." George cut him off.

"I'm sure. Okay. You think I'd part with my good luck charm now?" They drove slowly out of town and onto road to the farm. The storm had passed. Matthew gazed upward through the pickup window and as the clouds moved off like a parting curtain, revealing a sky of brilliant stars, glittering as only they can in the dark countryside on a clear, cold, crisp night.

"I guess you saw a lot over there," George remarked.

"Yes," Matthew answered in a soft, melancholy voice. He looked away from the stars at George.

"Lost friends, you said."

"Yes. A few. But just one hurts as much as all."

"How did you handle it? The grief I mean?"

"Alone. No one really wanted to know..."

"I do." George said. Matthew knew it was a genuine remark.

"Back home, I talked my way out of a lot of relationships. No one could really understand? I mean, how could they? And over there? We never had time to grieve. You meet guys... Get to know some... If you lost a friend, well, his body was medivacked out. You know - No one left behind. It was our credo."

"I know. It was the same with the 101. Not official, but we just did it."

"And then you keep going - do the mission,

cover your team, stay alive. No time to mourn. The enormity of death piled up and backed up. No time to reflect. Then that bill came due when we got home and had the time. It came bubbling up and out and..." Matthew took a deep breath, as if setting aside that burden. "I'll always remember them. But I guess you know about that, George." George leaned forward and looked up through the windshield at the brilliant sky.

"That I do. There are a few guys here who saw it all. We talk sometimes...well, they do. I'm with them about it. But with my John... well... to bury a child is painful beyond description. I think if it had been some other way, something natural, you know...an accident or illness, well then maybe I... we, might have accepted it better, if there is such a thing as accepting. And then, the capper was that we were notified on Christmas Eve... nineteen-ninety."

"That's harsh," Matthew said softly. "But, you know, they have to let you know as soon as possible. It's a rule. Family first."

"We'd just had a letter from John. He was supposed to be home by Christmas." The tree blocked George's view in the rear view mirror, and the road here had not been plowed for a few hours, so he drove cautiously. They passed homes and farmhouses with warm, cheery, Christmas lights that seemed to beckon to them out of the darkness.

"So that's why Christmas hasn't been... Now I understand," Matthew said.

"John said in his letter that they were leaving soon. 'Nothing to worry about, dad.' That's what he wrote. They told us he saved his team. Could've had a shot at being the last man out, but..."

"He did the right thing, huh?"

"John's unit was inside Iraq. Their mission was to find Scud missiles sites before they could be launched. John found a few of them, and then they ran into a Republican Guard Motorized Company - Saddam's elite. They were taking fire from three sides, lost one Black Hawk trying to get them out. A second Black Hawk came in and John got his team aboard. What they told us was that John grabbed an automatic weapon, turned, and went back to give covering fire to let his team make it."

"So he died buying time for the others," Matthew said quietly. "That's how we trained. That's what we did."

"They gave him a posthumous DSC. And like you said, no one gets left behind. They went back... brought his body home a few weeks later." Matthew nodded.

"You raised him well..." George pulled to the side of the road and stopped.

"I made myself believe that he did the right thing. But the truth is I never raised him to die. And his mother..."

"Some people just have to rise to occasions. Sometimes death is the price." They sat in silence for a moment. Matthew sensed George was struggling with something. He waited patiently.

"Matthew?" George finally began nervously. "I feel like I well...sort of know you. And I'd like to ask you to do something. If it sounds strange or anything, just forget I asked."

"What do you need?"

"It's for my wife and daughter. I think it could help if well...if you could let them believe you ran into John over there. That you knew him. I know it was long ago, and I really mean you don't have to, but..."

"No problem," Matthew said quickly. "I understand. I can do that. Actually, I was in the 5th SFG myself. We lost guys before the tanks rolled across the desert in Kuwait and Iraq. Black-ops. Not much said about it."

"So maybe you did know Johnny. He was a Staff Sergeant. A little shorter than me. Dark hair.

Medical Specialist. Here..." George reached into his pants pocket and took out his wallet. He handed a photograph of John to Matthew.

"That's my son," George said pointing to his son standing between two friends. "It was taken in Bahrain on R & R." Matthew studied the snapshot of John and his buddies. They were lean and hard looking, standing in front of the Intercontinental Hotel, wearing silky white shirts and touristy burnooses. He handed the photo back to George.

"I didn't know him.   Sorry." George nodded. It was a long shot.

"So doing this doesn't sound weird to you?"

"Not at all. If it's part of their healing, then it's my pleasure to help. What do you want me to know?"

"John's dog's name was Sport. You know that. Uh... and he was very protective of his little sister."

"Sounds like half the guys I knew."

"He had a scar on the top right side of his neck where she threw a toy at him once. And he played baseball for New Chatham High School..."

"Good stuff, George.   I'll be happy to..." Suddenly George's cell phone rang. He answered it and listened.

"Okay," was all he said, smiled, and clicked

off. Then George made a U-turn back toward town. "We've got to make a detour."

CHAPTER TWELVE

A FAMILY GATHERS

Neither man spoke as they drove back through the now deserted streets of New Chatham. This time they were on the far side of town, just a few miles from Chatham itself. They made their way to the town center, passing the war memorial park. Matthew gazed at the five columns of stone until they were no longer in sight as they turned off Main Street and down to the train station. The long low roof covering the station, waiting room and platform held a two-foot thick deposit of fresh snow. Tire tracks, where waiting cars parked earlier, had almost been erased by the last burst of the snow storm. A lone hatless figure of a man in a topcoat paced back and forth clutching overstuffed shopping bags in his arms. He stopped to stomp his feet against the icy platform in a pointless gesture to stay warm. George flashed his hi-beams as he pulled the pickup in close to the man, then parked with the engine running and got out.

"Hi Harold. Let me give you a hand."

"Thanks George. I wasn't sure if you'd want..." George took one of the shopping bags from Harold. He noticed it was filled with gifts.

"C'mon, Santa. It's Christmas Eve and there's a room at the Inn."

"I was freezin' my butt off..."

"It's warm in the truck." George led the way. Matthew had climbed into the narrow space behind the front seat. Harold and George got in.

"Hand me those bags," Matthew said. "There's room back here."

"Thanks." Harold handed the bags to Matthew. "And you are?" He asked, eyeing Matthew suspiciously.

"I'm Matthew." They shook hands. Harold's were ice cold.

"No gloves?" Matthew asked.

"Left them on the train. I fell asleep and...ah well, I'm warm now. I'm Harold," he gasped, trying to catching his breath. It must be the cold, he thought, and the heat in the truck.

"I see," Matthew said, being polite. He released Harold's hand. George, unaware of the exchange between Matthew and Harold, got into the truck.

"I'm glad you came," George said as he pulled out of the station parking lot.

"It was sort of a last minute thing." Harold was still drawing in air. He held his hands to heater vent.

"Maybe better that way," George said. "I know David'll be glad to see you. David is my grandson," George said over his shoulder to Matthew. "Harold here is... uh, was my son-in-law."

"How's she doing?" asked Harold.

"She's tired. Upset. Worried. Who wouldn't be?"

"I wanted to be here Monday, but she said no. She didn't want David around the hospital." George knew that.

He glanced quickly back at Matthew.

"My daughter had a lumpectomy on Monday. We don't really know what's what. But we'll know more after Christmas when the pathology comes back."

"I'm sure she'll be okay," Matthew said. He leaned forward and reassuringly tapped Harold on the shoulder. It seemed as though he could feel the warmth of Matthew hand through his heavy winter coat.

"I'm glad you came, Harold," said George. "I truly am. With you and David here it makes a family Christmas."

"Thanks, George. That's good of you to say."

Harold took his hands away from the vent. His breathing was easier now. "So who is Matthew?" he asked as if Matthew were not sitting behind him.

"A Christmas visitor. Unexpected. He'd like to froze to death if I hadn't come along."

"Like me?"

"No. He was hitchhiking in the middle of the storm. I nearly ran him over. Crazy! So it turns out he needs a place for the night, and we have room at the Inn, actually two rooms, so to speak." Harold nodded and smiled. He opened his coat buttons as the heater poured forth abundant warmth.

"Do you really think my coming up...I mean unannounced, is going to be okay?"

"I hope so," George answered. "Carol agreed to try to have Christmas - for David if for no other reason. I left them to get the tree lights and ornaments ready. You caught us in town getting a tree. Let's hope the spirit has them. If not, you just have to sleep in the barn. No trains back tonight."

"The barn? Jesus George..." George laughed aloud. He enjoyed teasing Harold, who was always a pretty serious study - a little short on sense of humor.

They drove the rest of the way home in silence.

George drew on the external trappings of Christmas along the way; the homes all lit with bright, cheery, welcoming lights, to stoke his inner warmth. Harold wrestled uneasily with thoughts of Jenny being furious at him and Carol taking her side. Beneath is all he was afraid for Jenny and not sure that David had totally forgiven him fro the Thanksgiving argument. Matthew calmly stretched out and gazed at the night sky.

When George turned into the driveway, and started down the steep slope toward the house, he slipped the transmission into low four-wheel drive. Harold took a deep breath, steeling himself for a possible confrontation. Matthew shifted in his seat and glanced at the surroundings.

"And here we are," George announced. He turned off the motor. For a long moment, the three men sat in silence. A breeze blew some snow, back-lit by the light from the house, across the walkway to the front door. He realized that Carol must have shoveled it. George put his hand on Harold's shoulder.

"Why don't you go on in and get your surprise over with? Matthew and I will bring the tree." He got out of the truck. Harold opened his door.

"Could you pass me those," he asked Matthew,

pointing to the gifts. Matthew passed the shopping bags to Harold, one at a time.

"It looks like there's gonna be one happy boy tomorrow morning," he said. "Kids and Christmas. Nothing like it."

"I hope so," Harold said as he climbed out of the truck. Matthew followed.

"Good luck," George said as he walked around to the rear of the truck.

"It'll be fine," Matthew said softly to Harold. As he walked up the stone path to the front steps, Harold wondered how this stranger, or at least that's what George said he was, felt he had to comment about the reception he was going to get. How did he know? He knocked gently on the door. Carol, who had heard the truck approach, opened it expecting to see her husband. The sight of Harold, holding the two large shopping bags of gifts, startled her for a moment, but she quickly recovered her composure. She had always liked him, but when it came to taking side, he was the outsider and Jenny washer daughter.

"Harold! What a surprise." She looked past him toward the truck. "How did you get here?"

"Train. I called George on his cell. He's getting the... He shivered. Uh...listen, Carol. Can I come in?"

"What? Oh dear... Of course. I'm sorry. It's just... You're such a surprise and I was expecting... of course. Come in. Come in." At that moment, as Harold stepped into the foyer, Jennifer came out of the kitchen into the living room. Their eyes met. She froze in her tracks. Harold quickly put down the presents and went to her. Carol followed, leaving the front door ajar.

"Jenny," he said, in a warm, friendly voice. "How are you?"

"What the hell are you doing here?" she responded, coldly. He hesitated.

"Well... It's Christmas and I uh... I thought I'd... I brought presents for you and the folks. And David, he should..." His voice trailed off. His eyes were cast down at the oak floor. Jennifer softened a bit, but maintained her defensive body language – stiff and leaning slightly backward from him.

"I see. Well, David's napping. The trip knocked him out. And if you were planning to come, why didn't you come with him? Then he wouldn't have had to make the trip alone."

"I didn't know...I mean it was a spur of the moment thing. I just... I suddenly knew had to come. I'm sorry, Jen." Jennifer glanced quickly at her mother, and then back at Harold. "You're dressed pretty formally for the country."

"And the snow. Like I said, it was last minute. I just... Well... Look Jen...I've been a jerk and I wanted to..." He looked around. Not the time or place for what he wanted to say to her. It was an awkward moment for all concerned.

"Would you like some hot coffee?" Carol asked, trying to settle things a bit. Her voice was pleasant. She saw that Jennifer was, in a way, glad to see her ex-husband.

"That would be great," Harold answered, relieved.

"Give me your coat," Jennifer said. She took it and hung it in the foyer closet.

A few minutes later, as Carol came out of the kitchen with Harold's coffee, she heard George directing someone to 'pull hard to the left'. Harold and Jennifer were in the living room next to the fire. David was napping upstairs. So who, she wondered, was George talking to? She handed Harold his coffee as she heard the front door bang open.

"What in God's name?" She walked quickly toward the front door just as it opened abruptly. George burst in with a broad smile on his face.

"Hiya beautiful," he bellowed with a wide grin. Then he turned and hauled the base of the tree into the foyer, spilling snow onto the floor. He kissed Carol on the cheek and hauled more of the large tree into the house.

"She's a beauty, honey. Just look at her!" As Carol examined the tree Matthew came through the doorway supporting the top of it. His B-4 bag was slung over his shoulder.

"And this is Matthew!" George announced with a flourish. "Matthew, my wife Carol."

"Hello, Carol. Merry Christmas." Carol was confused.

"Yes... Well, hello Matthew. Thank you. To you too." She threw a quizzical look at George.

"I found Matthew freezing on Mill Pond Road, love. Actually," he chuckled, "I nearly ran him over."

"It was snowing pretty hard, Mrs. Boyajian."

"He's heading home but his ride isn't coming 'til morning. So I invited him to spend Christmas with us. Okay?" George sounded like a little boy asking his mother if a friend could sleep over. Carol smiled to herself. Matthew's eyes met hers with an intuitive recognition.

"Of course it's okay." What choice do I have, Carol thought to herself? "Welcome to our home,

Matthew. I'm happy you're here." Carol extended her hand and Matthew accepted it with slight nod, and smile. Her touch was warm.

"I thank you kindly, ma'am." Jennifer and Harold walked into the foyer.

"Come say hello to Matthew," George said to his daughter. Matthew extended his hand. Jennifer accepted it.

"Nice to meet you Jennifer. Merry Christmas." Jennifer looked down at Matthew's hand and slowly pulled hers away. She shivered slightly. "Uh... Thanks. You too," she said, wondering how many more surprises this Christmas Eve would bring.

CHAPTER THIRTEEN

APOLOGIES

Matthew led the way into the living room, gripping the heavier base of the tree while George hefted the full top quarter behind him. Distracted, something had bothered George but he couldn't put his finger on it. Then, before he could tell Matthew where to go, the stranger guided the base of the tree to a position close to the bay window and set it down.

"That's where we always put the tree," Carol said. "How did you know?" Matthew shrugged.

"I didn't. It just seemed like the right spot."

"Help me walk this upright," George said to Harold.

"Just a second," Carol said to her husband. "Where's the base I told you to get?"

"Base? What base?"

"For the tree? With a water pan? I asked you not to forget to buy at Williamson's."

"Oh... That base. He was uh...closing and I didn't want to hold him up. But no problema. I'll make one." George headed for the back door. "I've got what I need in the shop." He closed the kitchen door behind him.

"Why does he never listen?" Carol said to Matthew, as though he knew. "Would you like something? Coffee? We have some nice cookies."

"Sounds great. Black please."

"I'll get it, mom," Jennifer said. She went into the kitchen. Harold followed.

"Please, Matthew. Sit down," Carol said. Matthew sat in the center of the sofa, facing the fire which was well established now, with a glowing bed of coals. Carol sat in one of the nearby wing chairs. "I hope you're not too hungry. We used to uh... that is, we always have dinner after we trim the tree."

"I ate on the road this afternoon, but there's always room for a home cooked meal." Carol smiled. She liked Matthew. There was something comfortable and calming about him - more like a friend than a stranger.

In the kitchen, Jennifer put a cup of coffee in the microwave to heat up while she opened the tin of Mary Simpson's cookies. David had made a small dent in them, but there were still plenty left. 'Two unexpected visitors,' she thought to herself. 'It's as though Mary knew we'd need these'.

"So how are you feeling, Jen," Harold asked, trying to be casual and yet concerned, which he was. He could not gauge her state of mind. She had not rejected his sudden appearance and thrown him out. Was that a result of Matthew, a stranger, being in the house? No, he remembered, Matthew hadn't come in yet when Jenny saw him with Carol. Maybe, as he hoped, she had softened her attitude toward him. The surgery must have put an awful strain on her. He was sincerely concerned. In fact, it was beyond just concern. He knew, from the moment he saw her this evening, that he still loved her deeply.

"I'm okay, I guess." Her tone of voice was sincere. He felt relieved. If she was going to cloud up and rain on him, or throw him out, this was the perfect time and place to do it - out of sight of parents, David, and the stranger. "I'm still a little tired," she volunteered. The microwave bell went off. Jennifer went to get the coffee, but Harold was closer.

"I'll get it." He went to the microwave.

"I'm not that tired," she snapped. Then her shoulders sagged, and she relaxed. "Sorry. Thanks."

"I'm sorry about not calling. I just had to come... to see you...to be with David. There so much I want to say..." The kitchen door burst open and George came in from the workshop toting a hammer, saw, nails, and several pieces of pine planking. His intrusion stopped Harold dead in his tracks. The discussion, their future and David's, would have to wait for a private, uninterrupted moment.

"Thank you," Carol said as Matthew stoked the fire and adding a log. "Where did you find that beautiful tree?"

"George found it. Next to the church. From Artie?"

"That old codger was still open? I thought, for sure, George would have to go to Chatham, or even Albany."

"I guess we were lucky. It's a great tree. And it seems to belong..." Suddenly, George came into the room, followed by Jennifer, who carried a dish of cookies, followed by Harold, with Matthew's coffee.

"I'm baaa-aak," George announced, mimicking the little girl in the 'Poltergeist' movie. "I'd best do this here rather than guess at the diameter of the trunk." He put his tools and wood down next to the tree, which was now leaning against the bay window.

"I did say to remember the base, didn't I?" Carol

asked her husband.

"Yes you did, love. I should have gone to Williamson's first. A senior moment. Forgive me?"

"For now, I'll take pity on an old man." She smiled playfully. George was glad to see her relaxed. It gave him hope that she would welcome Christmas again. "But you'll have to get one with a water pan or we'll have pine needles all over this house."

"Deal. Now, let's get this built so we can get started trimming this beauty." Matthew got up from the fire, ready to work.

"I've got to get onto dinner," Carol said, and left the room. Jennifer knew Harold wanted to continue their discussion. So did she.

"Dad," she said," I'm going up to check on David." She sneaked a look at Harold.

"Maybe if he's up I can say hello now," Harold said, picking up on her signal. He followed her toward the stairs. George picked up the first pine plank then looked around. He was missing something.

"Hang in a sec," he told Matthew. "I forgot my tape measure. I think Carol has a small one in the kitchen."

George found Carol staring into the refrigerator.

She seemed a little bewildered. He came up behind and put his arms around her.

"What's up, love?" She leaned back against his solid body - her rock.

"I was just taking a moment to catch my breath. I don't know if I can do this, George. And now, with Harold here... He seems to genuinely care."

"He loves Jenny. I feel that."

"Yes. He does, doesn't he? And Jenny seemed almost glad to see him, don't you think?" She turned to face her husband.

"Yes. I do. Maybe it's the power of Christmas at work." He smiled.

"Maybe it's your new friend. He seems very nice."

"Matthew? Yeah, he is. But a bit lost. Sort of a drifter."

"I thought you said he was going home to his family." "I don't know. He doesn't seem to want to talk about

it, so I let it go. Listen, do you remember my telling Matthew Jennifer's name?" Carol looked at him quizzically.

"You must have. He knew it." George wasn't sure.

"Funny. I just don't remember if..."

"Another 'senior moment'?" she teased. He laughed.

"I suppose so. It's okay that I invited him, huh? He's a nice guy. Seemed so alone." Carol smiled and closed the refrigerator, satisfied there would be enough for dinner.

"You're a pushover, George Boyajian. And I love you just that way." She kissed her husband on the cheek. "I'm delighted that you invited him. But I still don't know how I feel about doing all this. I sort of feel sad, George. I don't want to feel sad, but I do." He went to a drawer in one of the floor cabinets and rummaged around.

"What do you need?" Carol asked.

"Got it," he said, holding up a small tape measure. He popped it into his shirt pocket. "Listen. I've had lots of ups and downs over this too. Some of them were unbearably sad. Memories popping up. Larry when I bought the lights, and old Arnie and the tree."

"It's beautiful."

"Yes. It was a miracle he still had it." He took her hands in his. We're a family, Carol. We're together. We can do it. We can have Christmas again." He kissed her on the cheek and left. Carol opened the refrigerator again for another calculation of how to stretch dinner for two more hungry men. "Maybe we can have Christmas again," she echoed. "Maybe Matthew can help."

Upstairs, Jennifer tiptoed out of her room, and closed the door softly behind her. Harold was waiting in the hallway.

"He's out like a light."

"Let him sleep. I'll see him later." Jennifer nodded and leaned against the wall. Harold came to her side.

"You okay?"

"A little tired myself." He took her hand. She didn't resist, but her body stiffened. "Look Harold. I'm really vulnerable right now. I'll admit that. I can't do this alone. Mom and dad have been solid, but David is very worried. He asked me what would happen to him if I died."

"Jesus, Jen."

"At first I told him he would live with mom and dad."

"You what?" Harold felt a surge of anger, but he suppressed it. Jennifer quickly put her hand on his cheek.

"No. No. I'll be honest. I was angry. But that all passed and I told him that of course he would live with you. You're his father. I assured him he'd be okay." Harold relaxed and pulled her h and to his lips and kissed her fingers. She smiled. "Then he wanted to know what would happened to him if you died." Harold winced as though someone had hit him in the gut. He tightened his grip on Jennifer's hand.

"He's wise beyond his years."

"Yes. Sensitive. Anyway, I said none of this would ever happen, but if it did, he'd live here with Grandma and Grandpa. That seemed to calm him. We haven't talked about it since."

"Jenny? I want to say something to you." She looked into his eyes. They were watery.

"What?"

"Direct and honest? I'm sorry. I'm so very sorry. I never should have lost my temper in front of David and said those things that I said. I lost it. I just lost it when you talked about joining your brother. I'm a jerk, and I'm sorry." She knew he was sincere. Something about him had changed. He seemed to have matured overnight...Less self-centered. Warmer and open.

"You spoke about John as though he was some kind of enemy to you."

"In a way he was. But I had no right to say what

I did, especially in front of David. The fact is that I'm jealous of your brother."

"Jealous? But you never knew him."

"That's right. But he was all the things I'm not. Brave. Heroic. Sure of himself..." He paused. "Loved..." She reached up and touched his face.

"You were...you are, loved. Your son loves you. I know I did and..." She could not say any more. He understood why. His heart was beating like a kid on his first date.

"Well," he said, in hoarse whisper. "I wanted to... No, I needed to come up here to say that I am truly sorry, Jen. And that I never should have let you go." He pulled her hand up to his lips again and kissed it tenderly. She relaxed as calmness spread through her body. For the first time in weeks she felt warm and alive inside. She felt hope.

"David will be so glad you're here for Christmas," she said, gently pulling away her hand from his lips. And then an inner voice cautioned her not to take the conversation any further.

Twenty minutes later George finished nailing the sturdy, makeshift base. He was satisfied it would hold the tree.

"Okay, how about a hand." Matthew was sitting

on the sofa next to Jennifer who seemed more cheerful than she had in days. Harold was trying to organize the lights, ornaments, and tinsel that had been moved aside when the tree and unexpected guests had arrived. Matthew got up and took hold of the top of the tree. Together, he and George lifted it upright, setting it into the makeshift stand. It just cleared the ceiling.

"A perfect fit!" George exclaimed.

"A perfect tree," Jennifer responded. Just then, a still sleepy David appeared in the living room doorway. He saw the tree, then Matthew, and then his father. A lot had happened while he slept, and he was confused. But instinct took over and he ran to his father.

"Daddy!" he shouted. "Daddy's here!" Harold swept his son up in his arms and kissed his warm neck. He hugged David with a grip that announced to the world that he would never let him go.

CHAPTER FOURTEEN

STARLIGHT

George began the tree trimming with great ceremony. The first ornament to go on was an Armenian angel that his great grandmother had brought with her to America more than a century ago. It was a primitive looking trinket, carved from a piece of cherry wood and hand painted by Aram Boyajian, George's great grandfather, who had been killed by the Turks during the infamous Armenian massacres of the late nineteenth century. Millions died, but the Boyajians survived and escaped to flourish in America.

There was a ceremony the family had for the old angel. George took it and stood next to the tree. Carol joined him. She closed her eyes and raised her hand in the air. Then, like a Mystic holding some magical pointer, she let her hand float until, seemingly of its own accord, it stopped. With her eyes still closed she reached out and grasped the closest tree branch. George said that Great Grandma was guiding her, picking the spot. And so it was that the angel was hung. Everyone applauded. Then they all joined in, picking ornaments that Carol, Jennifer, and David had taken down from the attic and sorted earlier in the day. With each came a memory, a smile, a secret look, and questions about them from David.

"Why is this Santa so skinny, Grandpa?"

"It was from New Orleans, hand carved by a local Cajun artist. That's how she saw Santa," George answered.

"Who gave you this golden ball with flowers painted on it?"

"Grandma's sister, Great Aunt Pauline, brought it back from France in 1962."

"And who made this one that looks like an apple?" "Your mother made that in school when she was your age, David."

A while later, Matthew noticed that Jennifer had moved away from the activity and now sat near the hearth, on the floor in front of the fire. He put aside his handful of tinsel and joined her.

"Taking a break? he asked.

"Just resting."

"Mind if I join you?" She smiled and gestured

for him to sit down.

"So you're not from around here?" she asked as he settled in next to her.

"No. Just passing through."

"Then why do I think I know you?"

"I have that kind of face. Lots of people..." He was interrupted by a loud laugh from Carol. George was holding a most grotesque little ornament of a Leprechaun dressed as one of Santa's helpers.

"Oh dear God!" she exclaimed. "Your Aunt Bess' second husband Sean gave us that horrible creature."

"I remember. A housewarming gift," George said. "The first Christmas after we bought this place." He held the little gnome tenderly as David examined its face.

"You know Honey," George said seriously, "I always thought it looked like her first husband, Uncle Gene." Carol laughed.

"By God, it does. It actually does. She must have had him on the brain." Harold and David went back to work across the room trying to make sense of some strings of tree lights that had newly tangled when they were moved aside when the tree came in. Jennifer and Matthew went back to their discussion.

"It's one of those family things," she told him,

smiling. "You had to know Aunt Bess. She sort of collected husbands."

"I hear that. I guess most families have an Aunt Bess or two."

"Does yours?"

"Yes. But none her husbands were as handsome as that Leprechaun." Jennifer smiled. She liked this stranger. He was so easy to be with. He fit right in and exuded warmth that was different from that of the fire, for it warmed her inside.

Shortly after they'd hung the Leprechaun, there came a moment when Carol became self-conscious about her laughing, and the smile left her face. Was she being too jovial? Had the memory of John left so quickly on this anniversary night? She struggled with an inner conflict.

"What say we have a Christmas drink before we string the lights?" she suggested, feeling the need to take a break from Christmas. "I have some eggnog in the fridge."

"You do?" George was surprised.

"I picked up a bottle. I mean, I thought as long as you had your mind set on doing Christmas again..." She stopped in her tracks, and looked self consciously at Jennifer and Matthew.

"Matthew knows," George said softly.

"Oh," is all Carol said. She went into the kitchen, avoiding eye contact with anyone. She felt as if she were about to burst into tears. George saw how she was.

"I'll give you a hand," George said, as he followed her.

Jennifer and Matthew got up from the fire and surveyed the tree. It was nearly filled with ornaments and tinsel, ready for the lights.

"Most people do the lights first," Jennifer said, "but daddy likes to do them last." Matthew nodded.

"We did that too."

"He maintains that the tree shows you where to place ornaments best when it is bare, and then the ornaments tell you where to put lights to best show them off."

"Exactly. And what about this?" Matthew lifted a broken star from the coffee table. It was missing one of its five points.

"Oh that..." Jennifer said wistfully. "A long time ago that point broke off. It got lost. We used to joke about it, saying there were only four of us here, so it was okay to have only four points on the star." She turned back to examining the tree.

Matthew rummaged through a tall box of tangled old extension cords and unused lights that were impossible to unravel. It had been set aside because George's new lights more than replaced these. He pulled at the wires, separated them and their sockets, and reached deep into the box. When he pulled his hand out, he held the missing piece of the star.

"You mean this?" he asked Jennifer. Light from the fire shimmered on the lone star point's silver surface.

"How in the world did you...? Let me see." Matthew handed the broken fragment to her.

"I could have sworn that piece was lost...or thrown away...or...my goodness..."

"Do you have any glue?" Jennifer's eyes lit up.

"I think I can find some. Be right back." Matthew sat down on the sofa and examined the star and the missing piece. He played with fitting it together.

Meanwhile, in the kitchen, Carol had composed herself. She poured the eggnog into a blender while George washed and dried a silver tray, silver bowl, ladle, and crystal goblet set.

"You polished this silver, didn't you?" George shouted to her over the whirring of the blender. Carol nodded 'yes'. She turned off the machine and opened a bottle of Bacardi Anejo Rum – 80 proof. She contemplated how much to pour. She saw George was watching her.

"Is the whole thing too much?"

"So we'll get loaded," George said, chuckling.

"You? Mister straight and narrow? Loaded?" George smiled. There was a time, after John's death, when he drank far too much. Then one day he missed picking Jennifer up at dance class and that was the end of it. No AA or step program for him. When it came to his children George had all the self-motivation he needed.

"Well why not?" Carol said, reassuring herself that a drink or two would take the edge off the melancholy feeling she was experiencing. She poured in the whole bottle of the potent brown liquor, and flipped on the blender. The creamy eggnog mixed easily with the rum. After several seconds Carol poured the foamy, beige, mixture into the silver bowl. George picked up the tray. She put her hand on his arm.

"Just a minute." George knew that tone of voice. He put down the tray. "I want to tell you something Jennifer said today. Something about Christmas." George saw her lower lip begin to quiver. He took her hand.

"What is it, love?" He waited patiently as she gathered herself.

"She said Christmas... Oh, George... We were so... All those years, when we didn't have Christmas. She missed something precious. We were so caught up that..." Carol closed her eyes and shook her head slowly from side to side.

"What? Tell me," he asked softly.

"God help us, George, we took Christmas away from her. We wanted her to grieve as we did." George understood immediately. He nodded slowly and swallowed hard.

"We lost our only son, sweetheart."

"But we were so selfish." George placed his arms around Carol and hugged her to his chest.

"No my darling. Not selfish. Hurt. Blinded."

"And our blindness hurt her. Not to have Christmas like the other kids..." Carol paused. "You see, she thought we loved Johnny more than her... That we cared more about him... She came to believe that in our eyes, she didn't deserve Christmas."

"Oh dear. No." A flush of shame tore at his heart as tears filled George's eyes. "That poor girl. My God, what did we do?" Carol looked directly at him.

"Look. Please don't say anything to her. Not now. Not while everyone's here. Tomorrow we can talk it out quietly...Try to explain how we... I don't know."

"Spilt milk. I never thought to... What did we do? What did we do?" Carol gently stroked his grizzly face. He needed a shave.

"I believe now she understands."

"Still and all... You're right. Tomorrow I'll..."

"Yes. But now we have a tree to trim, guests to entertain, and a grandson who must have a proper Christmas." She kissed him. "I love you." Then he saw a twinkle in her eye that made his heart skip a beat. It was a glimpse of his Carol before John died. "Now, big boy," she joked, "grab that booze and let's party." George picked up the tray.

"Matthew's a nice man, isn't he?" George asked while she grabbed the silver ladle, still in the sink, and dried it.

"You know he looks about the same age that Johnny would have been..." Carol said as she slipped the ladle into the bowl.

"Yes. Listen uh...actually he...he knew John in Saudi..." Carol's face turned ghostly white.

"What did you say?"

"Saudi Arabia. Matthew was in Special Forces too. The same group. The 5th."

"Oh George. Are you sure?," Carol was

suspicious. "Maybe he made that up. You know... you hear stories about..."

"You think this guy's a con artist? No way. I felt good about him from the get-go. There's something really sincere about him. No Carol. He's good people."

"Okay. If you say so. Oh...Mary Simpson came by while you were out getting the tree. She brought some cookies... Let me put them out." She took the chocolate chip and butter cookies and arranged them in a fan pattern on the silver tray. She added a Pepsi for David.

"Happy?" he asked.

"Not sad," she answered softly. "Mary asked us to come to midnight service. What do you think?"

"Maybe. I know how Harold feels about it but maybe Jenny will want to take David." George and Carol stopped for a moment in front of the kitchen window. The moon had risen, full. They gazed out at the serene, snow covered, fields as they reflected the blue-white moonlight. "I didn't ask Matthew about it. We were next to the church when we got the tree from Artie but he didn't..." Carol touched George's shoulder.

"He reminds you of John, doesn't he?" she whispered.

"In a way. It's as if it wouldn't be Christmas Eve with just us... without another...a young man...you know what I mean?" She nodded.

"Mmmmmm... And what do you think about Harold being here?"

"I wasn't happy with him during the divorce. That's for sure. But it took guts for him come here. Maybe he's trying to show Jenny something. All I know is if it's going to work out, they've got to do it themselves."

"I agree."

George and Carol swept into the room, carrying the eggnog and cookies. They saw Matthew and Jennifer sitting close to one another on the sofa. Harold and David stood next to them.   Matthew was handing something to Jennifer.

"Here's the Christmas cheer," Carol announced brightly.

"Generously spiked," George added, "by Miss Heavy-hand."

"Oh George," Carol protested. "It was only two bottles of 151 proof Bacardi. These young people can take it." Everyone laughed at her joke. Jennifer stood up and showed her parents the star, now repaired with all five points in place.

"Look what Matthew did!" Carol gasped at the sight of the star, made whole again. She swayed slightly against George, who had to juggle the tray and support her. The star seemed to have brilliance beyond the reflection of the firelight and floor lamps in the room.

"How on earth...?" was all Carol could say.

"Where did you find the piece?" George asked.

"In a tall box. That one," Matthew said, pointing. "It was stuck in among the old wires and electrical stuff." He got up. "So," he said directly to Jennifer, "where shall we put it?"

"On the top, silly." Jennifer answered. "Where else would it go?"

"Right you are." Matthew looked around the living room for something to stand on. "We need a ladder."

"No. Just boost me." Jennifer said too quickly.

"Like this?" Matthew asked making a stirrup with his hands. It was all a stunning déjà vu for Jennifer. She stared at Matthew for a very long moment. An eternity...

"I uh... I mean...I think we'll need a real ladder," Jennifer said, still not sure of what she had just experienced, other than she felt she had relived a moment, verbatim, from long ago.

"Wait," Matthew announced. "I've got an idea." He climbed halfway up the stairs, held the banister with one hand, and precariously leaned out into the air over the tree. He stretched and placed the star on top of the tree. Everyone applauded.

"Now," George announced, "let's have a drink, or two,

and then get the lights in place. It's time we got this puppy fired up!"

CHAPTER FIFTEEN

A GIFT OF LOVE

An hour, and several eggnog's later, they were done. Mary Simpson's cookies were gone. Everyone, except of course David, was feeling mellow as they stepped back to admire their work. George, who had supervised the placement of the lights, was antsy to see the tree lit.

"You wanna do the honors, honey?" George said as he put his arm around Jennifer.

"No, dad. Let mom do it." George nodded at his daughter's wisdom. He handed the master switch to Carol.

"Hold one sec," he said. Then he turned off all the floor lamps so that all that illuminated the room was firelight. Carol's hand trembled a little.

"Come do it with me sweetheart," she said to David. She took his hand. His eyes were wide and sparkling with anticipation. "Okay," Carol said, "Ready? Here goes." She placed her hand over David's and snapped the switch. The tree exploded in a brilliant rush of color, sparkles, reflections, flickering, and pure wonder. Broad smiles appeared on everyone's lips, followed by a collective 'Ahhhh..." Then a huge "Wow!" came from David.

"Oh mom...dad... It's soooo beautiful," Jennifer said.

"Merry Christmas," Matthew said softly. George put his arm around Carol who was still holding David's hand.

"This is right," George said. He put his other arm around Jennifer, who was smiling up at Harold at her side. Jennifer slipped her arm through his. Harold stroked her hand as it settled in the crook of his arm. Matthew noticed the gesture, and smiled to himself. The tree's light mingled with the firelight. The gentle snap and hiss from the fireplace added a warm, comforting, sound as the group stood before the tree. Silently, each in their own way remembered Christmas, and John, in a silent prayer.

It took another twenty minutes to add the tinsel to the tree – the final touch. George supervised while he sipped his fourth eggnog. Carol was a little concerned that George was drinking too much, but he seemed to be steady and in control, so she kept quiet. Maybe, as she had felt the need, this was also his way of getting through the evening. When they were done everyone sat down to admire their work.

"This brings back so many memories," Jennifer said.

"Good memories," George added softly.

"Yes," Carol said hesitantly. There was a slight touch of melancholy in her voice.

"Tell us about John," George said to Matthew, who sat near the fire with David.

"John?" Jennifer said, looking from her father to Matthew. "You knew my brother?"

"Yes." David didn't quite understand. He frowned.

"You knew my Uncle John?" he asked.

"Yes, David."

"But how?" Jennifer asked again. She was sitting at Harold's side on the sofa and got up.

"Our paths crossed in Saudi Arabia. I was in the 5th Special Force Group too."

"Can you tell us about it. Please." Jennifer begged.

"Well... We were in different units, but when we first got to Saudi we were at the same assembly area. Getting our desert issue. Going to Op's briefings. The same mess. Like that... In the beginning, while things were getting organized, we had some time on our hands. We were out in the boonies, far from

Riyadh. It was a God-forsaken place. Hot as blazes. Barren. Just desert. By ten in the morning you couldn't touch anything metal. Like in those old World War Two Africa Corps newsreels? I mean you could crack an egg and fry it on a Hum-Vee fender."

"Did he ever talk about me?" Jennifer asked. She was only interested in hearing about John.

"Oh yeah," Matthew said quickly. "Like he had this doll of a little sister, and how when you were older, he was going to have to keep the guys away from you." Jennifer smiled and wiped a tear.

"Little as I was, John always teased about having a test for any boy who wanted to take me out. He said every girl's big brother did that."

"That's true," Matthew said. "I remember one story..." he looked directly at Jennifer. "John had this scar on the back of his neck? I asked him about it 'cause I thought he'd been wounded or something... you know? It didn't tan. He said you got mad at him for teasing you so you threw a toy at him." Jennifer smiled and nodded.

"Yes...I did that." George was glad he had asked Matthew to do this. He could see the connection it made for everyone. Carol was smiling. David listened with rapt attention. Even Harold was mesmerized by Matthew's recollections. It was as though he was finally meeting his late brother-in-law, albeit posthumously.

"Oh yeah... I remember we talked about baseball. I think he said he played for the High School."

"Yes. He surely did." Carol spoke up. There was pride in her voice. "He was very good."

"I remember he talked about the big game..."

"The State Championship – Division C. It was against Middletown." Jennifer said.

"He hit a home run in the last inning..." Carol added with even greater pride. He won the game for us!"

"Was my Uncle John a good soldier?" David asked. Everyone was surprised by the question coming from the ten year old. Matthew knelt down to David's height. He put his hand on his shoulder.

"He was the best, David. A darned good medic too. All the guys in his unit called him 'Doc'. They trusted him. They knew if they were ever hurt, he would take good care of them. He even told me that after his hitch was up he was thinking about going into medicine."

"My John? A doctor?" Carol said, with wonder in her voice. Her memory of a young boy in uniform didn't connect with an image of a man in a white lab coat ministering to patients in a hospital. When a child dies so young it is hard, if not impossible, to imagine them older.

"Yes ma'am," Matthew answered. "It seemed like he had the calling...and the talent. He would have been a fine doctor."

"Anything more about me?" Jennifer asked, hungry for contact with her brother. Matthew gazed out of the window at the snowy fields.

"I remember he talked about one winter... It was so hot there in the desert, we dreamt about everything cool or cold. He said he was dragging you along in a sled. You were laughing and screaming because he as going so fast. You fell off and then made a snow angel. He did too. He said you loved being a snow angel." Startled, George dropped his goblet. It broke into five large pieces on the living room floor. Carol quickly grabbed some paper napkins and knelt to clean the mess. She carefully picked up the glass first.

"Oh George... We've had those goblets such a long time."

"How in the world?" George muttered softly.

"How?" Carol answered. "That's your fourth eggnog, that's how." Carol smiled at Matthew. "I told you he can't drink." George was confused, and a little woozy.

"No. I mean how did he..." He looked at Matthew who was smiling at him. The young man had his arm around David.

"Oh well," Carol said, "It's only a glass." She put the wet napkins and shards on the tray. "Tell us more about John," she said. Matthew took a sip of his eggnog. Firelight, mixed with tree's brilliance, reflected in, and off, the facets of his crystal goblet. It softened his weathered face and hands. His dark eyes were serene.

"We really only met a few times. He was a leader. The rest of his team liked him, respected him. But," he sighed, "It was a long time ago. I'm sorry I don't remember more." There was a long moment of silence in the room.

"Hearing you talk about him," Carol finally said, "makes him seem somehow... I don't know... Closer, if that's possible." Jennifer went to the mantle. She took the picture of John and handed it to Matthew.

"I remember John like this. Desert Storm never was, like, part of my world back then. But your talking about him actually being there... your seeing him... knowing him... Well it somehow makes him more real to me. Not a memory, but a person again. Do you know what I mean?"

"Yes," Matthew answered, looking up at her from the picture. "I'm glad to have been able to do that."

"It fills in a time and place when I... we didn't know him," Carol added. "Thank you Matthew."

"You're most welcome. I'm sorry I couldn't tell you more..." Again, silence filled the room. Then Carol rose and picked up the tray, empty bowl, and the broken goblet.

"George? Can you bring this into the kitchen? I've got a ham in the oven, and a dinner to prepare."

"Can do, hon." George gathered the rest of the goblets and plates and stacked them precariously on the tray. "I'm starved," he announced.

"You have that tray under control?" Carol asked.

"Like a rock." He hefted it onto his shoulder like a seasoned waiter. "Remember...I worked those Catskill resorts for three summers as a kid."

A moment after George and Carol went into the kitchen, the headlights of a car flashed across the living room window.

"More company?" Jennifer questioned as she went to the front door. The few sips of eggnog and the pain killers she had taken earlier, plus the euphoria of hearing about her brother, had made her a little light headed and giddy. But when she opened the front door, a blast of cold air brought her back to reality. She saw a small, green two-door import pull in next to George's pickup. A woman got out of the car. As she walked up the path toward the door, Jennifer realized it was Elizabeth Meyers, John's high school girlfriend. She carried a small, gaily wrapped box in her hand. She waved to Jennifer when she saw her standing in the doorway.

"Oh my God!" Jennifer exclaimed. "Elizabeth!" She hugged the young woman like a long lost friend. Even though he isn't physically here, she thought to herself, so much of John is in this house tonight. "It's so good to see you, Liz. Come in. Come in." Jennifer closed the door. "Let me have your coat. Merry Christmas. My God, it's been what? Ten years?"

"Almost. Merry Christmas to you too. I'll keep my coat. I only stopped by to give your mom something. I'm staying with my aunt in New Chatham, and she's insisting that I go to church with her." Jennifer was disappointed.

"Oh? Well, okay. Come in. Mom's in the kitchen. I want you to meet my son..." Jennifer led Elizabeth into the living room. The tree was still the main source of light.

"Oh my. It's so beautiful," Elizabeth said as she stepped into the room. "I saw it from the driveway, but in here...wow!" Jennifer introduced Elizabeth to David, Harold and finally, Matthew. As she shook hands with Matthew, their eyes locked and she lingered for just a moment.

"Do I know you?" she asked.

"I don't think so," he said, glancing over at Jennifer. "I've got that kind of face, I'm told..."

"Chicago?" she persisted. "I lived there for seven years. East Elm Street. Near the lake?"

"No. My loss. I've never been there." He released her hand, but the sensation of his warm touch lingered. Carol came into the room carrying cheese, olives, pate' and crackers on a tray.

"Hor'doeuvres," she announced. Then she saw the latest visitor. "Elizabeth! What a surprise." She put down the tray of goodies and hugged Elizabeth. "Oh my... It's so good to see you. You look wonderful. Of course you'll stay for dinner."

"Thank you, but I can't. Sorry. Like I told George, I've got to go to church with my aunt and..."

"George knew you were coming?"

"He invited me for a drink. Didn't he tell...?" Carol looked puzzled for a moment, then grinned. "Maybe. These senior moments. They seem to happen more and more often."

"You two. Seniors? Never," Elizabeth said. Carol accepted the compliment gracefully.

"Thank you. But you must come by for dinner soon."

"I will. I'll be staying for a while. This is for you." Elizabeth handed her the small gift box.

"What this?"

"Something that I kept all these years. But I feel it belongs here." Carol untied the green ribbon, neatly tied over cherub and angel paper. She found a small blue Tiffany box in which a man's pocket watch nestled in blue velvet.

"Oh my," Carol said. Her hands trembled as she carefully lifted it out of the box. "How lovely. But why?"

"Look on the back," Elizabeth said softly. Carol turned the watch over and saw an inscription. It read, 'Home For Christmas – Our love is for always, Lizzie and John'. "I bought that for John. We were going to... we talked about getting engaged." Her hands trembled and her eyes closed, sending tears down her cheeks. "I was going to give it to him that Christmas when..." She couldn't finish the sentence. Carol hugged Elizabeth as both women openly wept.

"Thank you," Carol finally said. "This is a

beautiful... just a beautiful thing to do... For all of us." Elizabeth nodded and wiped her tears. She felt freed from a burden carried for a decade – a secret now finally told. "We would have been very proud to have you as our daughter-in-law."

"Thank you," Elizabeth said. Jennifer took the watch from her mother. She showed it to David and Harold. Matthew stood near the fireplace, an interested observer. At that moment George came in and greeted Elizabeth. Jennifer showed the watch to George. He was emotionally shaken. He hugged Elizabeth, in his own mind, apologizing for John's absence. She sensed that and patted him on the back to comfort him. Carol took it all in.

"Elizabeth? Now I'm going to insist you have a bite with us. Call your aunt and blame me. It's only seven-thirty. You can be back in plenty of time for midnight services." Elizabeth saw that Carol would not take no for an answer.

"Okay," she relented. "I'll call."

"Good! Now how about a drink? Red wine or white?"

"Red please."

"I'd offer you eggnog, but George drank it all." Carol rushed off to the kitchen before George could defend himself. Everyone laughed.

Elizabeth removed her coat. Jennifer took it to the foyer

closet. Harold and David continued to examine the watch.

George went into the dining room to set another place for dinner. Elizabeth stood alone. She made eye contact with Matthew. She smiled, and he smiled back.

"Merry Christmas," he said. "The watch is beautiful.

"Thanks. And Merry Christmas to you."

"C'mon by the fire. It's nice and warm."

"So who are you?" she asked as she joined him. "A friend of the family?"

"Sort of," he answered. "Just passing through. And you?" She felt very comfortable with him. Her answer flowed easily from her heart.

"Their son John and I were in love. We were going to get engaged after he came home. He didn't. I guess maybe you know that..."

"Yes," Matthew said as he glanced at John's picture on the mantle. "He talked about you." Elizabeth stiffened. A chill traveled up her spine.

"What did you say?"

"I uh...I knew him in Saudi Arabia. We were in the same outfit. You know... guy talk."

"So that's why you're here. You knew John."

"I did, but that's not how I came to be here. I was hitching... George picked me up. Just a coincidence." Elizabeth stared into Matthew's warm, brown, eyes.

"I believe nothing is this world is coincidence. It's all part of a grand plan that we know little about."

"Really?"

"Yes. Your being here... this family celebrating Christmas for the first time in years... This beautiful tree... it's all part of the plan."

"Like the watch?" he asked. She was taken aback for a moment, then smiled.

"Yes," she answered. "That too, I imagine. That too..."

CHAPTER SIXTEEN

A HEALING VOICE

Dinner was filled with small talk, as though everyone was trying to make believe that celebrating this night was a normal event in this house - everyone except David who kept asking questions about his Uncle John.

"Grandpa, did he play the infield? "

"Second base."

"Elizabeth, what did he wear to the prom?

"A powder blue dinner jacket and white pants."

"Mommy, can we make snow angels tomorrow?"

"Of course, darling."

"Can we make them in the same place you made them with Uncle John?"

"Yes we can."

"Matthew, did Uncle John shoot any enemy?"

Before Matthew could answer, George spoke up.

"He did David - in order to save his buddies."

They were all hungry, and magically, Carol managed to stretch everything to accommodate the three extra guests at the table. Even Jennifer had a good appetite, which pleased her parents who had watched her languish after the surgery. They talked about the way the town was growing; living in the new millennium and how the world seemed to have gone a little mad since it arrived; 911 and a trip that George made down to "ground zero" with some friends from the American Legion hall; the commercialization of Christmas; the pros and cons of city versus country living.

No one wanted dessert, except David. The eggnog and cookies had satisfied their craving for sweets. Carol served decaf hazelnut coffee, and David got some homemade vanilla ice cream that Carol had in the freezer. Time passed quickly and suddenly it was nearly nine-thirty. Elizabeth said she had to get going. It was a twenty-minute drive back to New Chatham, and her Aunt was always early for church. She said her good-byes to the Boyajian family. Carol gave her a long, loving hug, and insisted she call in a few days and come by for a long, catch-up, chat.

"And thank you ever so much for the watch," Carol whispered in Elizabeth's ear before she backed away. "I know what meant to you. It was a beautiful gesture. I will cherish it." Jennifer got Elizabeth's coat and they hugged good-bye at the front door. As Elizabeth started down the path toward her car, Matthew came into the foyer.

"I just remembered something John said about her," he told Jennifer. "I'll be back in a minute." Coatless, Matthew trotted down the snowy path and caught up with Elizabeth just as she was getting into her car. She was deep in thought and his voice startled her for a moment.

"Hi," he called out. "I uh... I just remembered something that maybe you'd like to hear." Elizabeth studied the man as he came closer. He was not handsome, but rugged and masculine. Sexy too, she thought. I could go for him. But it was his voice that charmed her. It sounded somehow familiar and comforting. And that was eerie.

"What's that?" she asked eagerly, as he stopped in front of her. He threw that disarming smile at her. The cold night air seemed to warm around them.

"I remembered one night, after a briefing. John and I were walking back to our assembly area. It was desert cool and there were a billion stars out. Like tonight." They both looked up at the brilliant Milky Way – a sparkling canopy of heaven above them. "It's even more spectacular out there - in the desert. No lights and all that."

"I can imagine," she said. Her gaze drifted back to him while he was still looking up. Then he looked at her. A pulse of adrenaline surge through her body. For a moment she felt his presence within her body – in her soul.

"John said he was going to marry you. He said that he loved you dearly. Deeply. With all his heart and might and soul." Elizabeth took in a deep breath, more a gasp, and held it as though she were absorbing his very words into her heart. He reached out and touched her hand.

"He knew you loved him too." He withdrew his hand. "That's all. I uh...remembered that he said it, and I wanted you to know... I mean that he felt the same way as you did. He said, that starry night, that if he didn't make it back, he was glad that he knew love, and that it was with you, and that he would love you forever." Elizabeth was overwhelmed by this stranger's kindness. But she was not going to cry, and that surprised her. Inwardly, she wondered 'why?', and then realized that the words she had just heard had come to her, from John, after more than a decade. If ever a case was to be made for a Grand Plan, this was it. Now she knew that John was watching over her, with love. She knew, in her heart, that she would see him again. That they would be together. She then reached out and put her gloved hand over Matthew's bare hand.

"Thank you, Matthew. More than I can say. God bless you." He released his grip. She got into her car. They exchanged one more knowing look, and then she drove away.

"Merry Christmas," he said aloud, but she was gone.

When Matthew returned to the house he found Jennifer alone in the living room, settled back on the sofa in front of the fire. He heard Carol and George in the kitchen, dealing with the dishes.

"Did you get her?" Jennifer asked.

"Yes. Where's everybody?"

"Mom and dad are in the kitchen, with strict orders for no one to offer to help. Harold took David up to bed. He tired – they both are. And David is so excited about Christmas - the presents of course. Harold said he'd lie down with him for a while until he went to sleep. Elizabeth is nice, isn't she?" Matthew noticed that Jennifer was very chatty, as though she was trying to avoid thinking about something.

"Very," he said as he sat down next to Jennifer.

"The fire's still going nicely."

"Daddy stoked it, and I added those logs a few minutes ago. Yes. Elizabeth was like family, and after John..." She smiled at Matthew.

"I miss him tonight."

"I know."

"Well anyway, Liz was here a lot. But then she went off to school and then got married and moved to Chicago and all that... so I guess people just drift away sometimes..."

"Life must go on for the living," Matthew said. There was along pause. "Your folks are fine people," he said, looking at the fire.

"Yes," she answered; her gaze in the same place. The rejuvenated fire licked at the dry Maple splits with a vengeance. "How about your family? What are they like?"

"They were much the same. Middle class. Hard working. Honest. Fun..."

"You don't want to talk about them, do you?"

"Well... It's painful for me. I hope you understand."

"I do. Like us with Johnny I suppose." Matthew nodded. They sat quietly again for a moment.

"Once we got this puppy,' Jennifer suddenly said as her need to talk returned. "He was a Yellow

Labrador Retriever. Johnny named him Sport. He'd just been weaned. I remember that first night we put him in the kitchen, in a box with a blanket and newspaper all around. He cried so loud that no one could sleep."

"Puppies are like that," Matthew said.

"I mean mom and dad tried everything - a radio, a ticking clock, even a Lawrence Welk tape. Nothing worked. Finally, John took Sport up to his room, into his bed. And little Sport went right to sleep. After that he never left Johnny's side. Those two... They were inseparable. Sport died four years ago. Daddy buried him out back... He wanted to put him next to Johnny, but the cemetery... you know."

"Yeah. A boy and his dog. There's nothing more beautiful." Jennifer just nodded.

"He told daddy he planned to go to college. After... you know," Jennifer said in a whisper.

"Yes."

"Oh. That's right. Medical school, you said."

"A lot of us had big plans... For after..." Jennifer suddenly winced in pain and reflexively reached in her pocket for a prescription drug vial. Matthew gently placed his hand on hers.

"You don't need that."

"Oh yes I do," she said firmly.

"Listen to me.   Try something else first."
Jennifer felt something in Matthew's voice that was
compelled her to listen. She slipped the vial back
into her pocket. "Now, close your eyes," he told
her.   Jennifer hesitated, then leaned back against
the sofa pillow and closed her eyes.   "Now take a
long, deep breath," Matthew said, his words were
hushed, but positive. Jennifer breathed deeply. "Let
it out slowly.   Keep your eyes closed and think of
something that would give you pure joy." Jennifer
strained to concentrate. Gradually her facial muscles
relaxed. She saw her son David running with Sport,
playing ball with him as John had done nearly
every day. "Good. Now hold onto that thought."
Matthew placed his hands on Jennifer's shoulders
and closed his eyes. Her body relaxed more. She
sighed deeply. The pain began to drift away. What
seemed like only a moment passed, and Matthew
withdrew his hands. Jennifer opened her eyes. The
pain had gone.

"That's a great trick."

"You won't need that prescription anymore."

"Well, I don't know about that, but I do feel...
Mmmm...sort of nice, but a little tired. If you'll
excuse me I think I'll go upstairs and check on the
boys... maybe nap for a while myself."

"Sounds like a plan." He stood, took her hand, and helped her to her feet. They were close for a moment. Their eyes met - an unspoken, trusting friendship between them was sealed. After she went upstairs, Matthew leaned back into the sofa and stared into the fire.

Carol hand-washed the dishes while George put away the remains of the dinner, and straightened up the dining room. Then she and George dried the dishes together - a set of Grandma's fine bone china. Carol would never put them in the dishwasher.

"He's really a nice man," she said. George, was lost in thought.

"Huh?"

"Matthew?"

"Oh, yeah. Very nice."

"I'm glad he's here. Did I say that before?"

"Yes."

"Well, I am. He seems to fit right in with Jenny and David. Even Elizabeth seemed to warm to him immediately."

She stopped drying and looked directly at George. "You're awfully quiet."

"Me? I'm just happy. I feel like we got over some kind of big hurdle. Don't you?" She hesitated, giving his question serious thought. With all the activity, guests, tree trimming and dinner, Carol hadn't really taken time to examine her real feelings. She had been so against this, and now... well... They had talked about John, and for the most part, it hadn't made her sad. Especially when Matthew spoke about knowing him. What had she been so afraid of? Forgetting John? Pushing him back into the past? No she thought. Maybe just finally facing that void and knowing it would never be filled, especially with anger, or self-pity, denial or blame.

"I think it's okay...that I'm okay," she finally said.

"I'm just not totally there yet." Then, in a special rush of great love for George, she kissed him on the lips. "But I'm glad you insisted," she said, "and I love you very much." Just after that, Matthew came into the kitchen carrying two coffee cups.

"These are the last of everything," he said, placing them in the sink.

"Where's Jennifer?" George asked.

"She went upstairs. She was tired." George put down his towel.

"I'll go look in on her."

"I think she's uh... Harold was going to lie down with David until he fell asleep. They may be..." But concerned, George was already out of the kitchen. Matthew picked up George's towel and started to dry a serving plate.

"You don't have to do that," Carol said.

"I'd like to." While Carol washed the two cups and saucers Matthew dried and stacked dishes on the kitchen table.

"I know George told you about... Why this is our first Christmas in a long time?"

"Yes he did. I guess we're all capable of building prisons for ourselves with memories." Carol gazed out of the kitchen window at the snow-covered landscape. The moon shone bright, casting a blue-white aura on the fields, and outlining the dark woods beyond.

"To get such news on Christmas Eve..." Carol whispered to herself.

"There are procedures they have to follow."

"I suppose... Still and all, the damage was done for a long time."

"Your sadness came from love... For John." Matthew's eyes met Carol's as she turned toward him.

"And loss," she added. "Incalculable, overwhelming loss. A child gone before a parent leaves an emptiness that can never be filled."

Matthew understood.

"But should his memory be such a bitter legacy? Would John want you to feel so empty? I don't think so. I think he'd want you all to have many wonderful memories of him and to be living fully, and with joy." Matthew gestured to the moonlit scene outside the window. "Like out there. Light and dark. The moonlight touches the snow and becomes a part of its beauty." Carol looked outside as he spoke. "The darkness of the night is also its light. What do you see out there? The night or the moonlight? Or both? Can you separate them? Should you?" Carol wasn't sure where he was going with this metaphor. "No, you shouldn't, because it's all one." He moved closer to Carol and whispered. "When death takes someone you love, it doesn't mean they aren't with you. You have to find them again... In a different way. John is here... In this room... In this house... In your heart... In your love. He's everywhere. You'll always have him Carol. Always." His words lifted her spirit, and she saw her loss clearly. Perhaps for the first time her trepidation about finally accepting her loss was gone. Tears welled up in her eyes. She gently touched Matthew's weathered face, then softly kissed him on the cheek.

"Thank you," she said. "Thank you so much."

"Merry Christmas," Matthew said with a broad grin.

CHAPTER SEVENTEEN

A GIFT FROM CHRISTMAS PAST

George appeared in the kitchen doorway. He wore his mackinaw, and had changed to heavy winter boots.

"Jennifer's sleeping in her room with David," he announced. "In for the night, I think. She looks right peaceful." He had Matthew's jacket in his hand.

"And Harold?" Carol asked.

"Watching TV in the guest room. I set him up with a towel. There was bedding already there."

"Oh, right. I made it up in case she wanted David to sleep by himself... or maybe...I don't know," Carol said. George grinned.

"Don't rush things. So? You guys done in here?" George asked.

"Just about." She eyed Matthew's jacket. George was up to something. "I'll finish up," she said.

"Okay," George said, handing Matthew his jacket. "C'mon. There's something I want to show you." Matthew put on his jacket and followed

George out the kitchen door, into the winter night. They trudged through the deep snow toward the barn. Their route was lit by the full moon, now almost directly overhead.

Across the field Matthew noticed a herd of foraging deer back away cautiously to the edge of the woods. They were all doe's.

"I'll bet there's a big buck lurking nearby," George commented as they reached the barn. He unlatched half of a wide double door, and slid it open. When they stepped inside George flicked a wall switch. This was his carpentry workshop – his private sanctuary and playroom. The shop was extremely well equipped, and organized. Several 'works in progress' lay about on benches and work tables.

"This is great," Matthew said sincerely. "When I was growing up my Dad had a shop like this. I used to love working in there...making things... hammering and sawing away."

"John too," George said as he looked around. He often pictured his young son at a workbench, tool in hand, attempting to build something like his father did - something that would please his father. Matthew opened his jacket. He breathed in the air – wood, glue, paint, and machine oil, all blended into a mixture that unmistakably said, 'This is a man's workshop.'

"This is really good work, George," Matthew said as he rubbed his hands across a small teak chest.

"My own design. I've built, let's see, eight or nine of them, I think. I did one for old Artie, the tree guy?"

Matthew moved through the shop. Walnut kitchen cabinets, a maple sideboard, an elaborate doll house... Then, as if drawn by a magnet, Matthew zeroed in on an object in the corner; a box, partially hidden with a dusty cloth.

"What's under here?" he asked.

"Why did I know you'd find that? It was a Christmas present for John." George paused before the box for a moment, as if he were afraid to touch it. He picked up a large 'C' clamp, and as he spoke he nervously, he twisted and turned the clamp in his hands. "I started it near the end of John's tour. I had a calendar here, like he had over there. It was sort of a race against time, and a distraction - me working out here every night past mid-night so I could check off the next day the moment it arrived. John over there, doing the same, I imagine." Matthew nodded.

"All the guys... the short-timers did that."

"We were going to wait to celebrate Christmas

until he got home. Want to see?" George asked, finally gathering the courage to look at what was under the cloth.

"It would be an honor," Matthew said. George removed the cloth, revealing a beautiful mahogany chest of drawers, with gleaming brass hinges and drawer knobs.

"Oh man, George. It's beautiful." Matthew stroked the richly finished chest with more a caress than a touch. "Really magnificent."

"The best work I ever did, son." Matthew smiled to himself. "Jesus. I uh... You don't mind I called you son, do you?"

"Not at all." George placed the dust cover back over the chest. "It's an heirloom you've created there. What will you do with it?"

"I never gave it much thought that went anywhere. An heirloom you say?" Matthew nodded. "Maybe I'll give it to Jenny...and she'll give it to David..."

"And it will be a gift from you to your family for generations. I bet John would love that idea." George just nodded. He had to give it more thought. The truth was that he didn't want to part with the chest. Maybe he felt that as long as he kept it John might return some day to claim it.

"I was afraid it wasn't going to be ready in time,"

George said, "but, you see, it turns out I had all the time in the world. Two lifetimes actually - his and mine." George adjusted the cloth cover. His voice quavered a bit. "I told you it was Christmas Eve when they uh..."

"Yes." George came back to the bench.

"It was like I had a bird locked in my heart. And when I saw those two - that young Major, and the Chaplain... Oh, Lord..." He was reliving that terrible moment, as he had, again and again, every silent Christmas Eve. "Something pried my heart open and that bird escaped and tore away a piece of my...and what was left hurt so much, and I knew I'd never have it back... Never." George opened a drawer above the workbench and carefully removed a rectangular glass-covered frame. He placed it on the bench. "They gave us these," he told Matthew. The younger man peered over George's shoulder. The frame contained a Distinguished Service Cross, Combat Infantryman's Badge, Bronze Star, Purple Heart, Air Medal, Southwest Asian Service Medal, Kuwait Liberation Medal, and the National Defense Service Medal. George pointed. "That's a DSC - from Congress."

"I know," Matthew said. His voice was barely audible.

"We gave them John, and they gave us these in return." George sobbed. "I keep it here because ... well, Carol won't have it in the house to remind her... But maybe now, after tonight... maybe..." He sobbed again, and turned away, ashamed of his tears. Matthew placed his hand on George's shoulder to comfort him. George took a handkerchief from his pocket and dried his eyes.

"Darn, I'm not usually like this. I got over the tears years ago. Must be Christmas, or something." He smiled weakly, knowing, feeling that it was not necessary to make excuses to this man, to whom he had just poured out his heart.

"You've made a good life here, George. Something to be proud of."

"Yes. We have. Doing Christmas again is much tougher than I'd imagined, but I knew it was time." He wiped his eye and gathered himself.

"I think it's great that you did." George studied the stranger. He had a question troubling him.

"Let me ask you something, Matthew. I told you some things about John...you know, when I asked if you would say that you knew him." Matthew nodded. "The scar that Jenny gave him wit they toy. I like the way you told it. But the baseball thing...I mean how did you know it was a home run and the

State Championship?"

"I didn't, George. It was Carol and Jennifer who talked about those things. I only said John talked about playing ball." George's recollection was fuzzy. Darned egg nog. Why had he let Carol put that whole bottle of rum into it?

"Oh...yeah. I guess so. But there was something else I didn't mention. At least I don't think I did. The snow angels. Did I?"

"No. But you have winters up here and lots of snow. I grew up that way too and we always made snow angels. Every kid does. So I just figured... I don't know. It seemed like it being Christmas Eve and all..." George nodded and understood.

"I want to tell you something, Matthew." He took a deep breath. "Both Carol and I agree that somehow your being here has made it easier. Like you belonged here."

"Thank you. That's really nice to hear. To belong somewhere... again." Without saying it, both men knew it was time to leave. George put the medal frame back in its private place of honor, then they both walked toward the door.

"Listen," George said as they reached the door, "One more thing. Did I tell you Jenny's name when we were in the truck?"

"No. I think Harold mentioned it after we picked him up."

"Oh. That's it. I thought I hadn't. Ahhh...getting old has its drawbacks." He chuckled.

"There's nothing old about you." George smiled and patted Matthew on the back. He opened the door to the workshop, and after Matthew was outside, turned off the light and slid the door shut. It seemed to have gotten colder. They both clutched the collars of their jackets closed.

The deer had moved back into to the field next to the barn. As they walked toward the house the Christmas tree, framed in the living room window, glowed brightly - a bold splash of color exploding in a blue, black, and silver, nightscape.

Carol was upstairs gathering some bedding and a towel for Matthew when she heard the TV still on in the guest room. She knocked gently on the door.

"Come in," Harold said. Carol opened the door. It had once been the nursery, used for both her children. Then it became an office for George's papers, contracts and plans, before he moved everything down to the barn. They had fixed it up as a guest room, but they rarely had guests, so it became a catchall storage room instead. Harold was lying on the bed, still dressed, with his shoes off.

"I hope I'm not disturbing you," Carol said, feeling
strange that her daughter's ex-husband was sleeping in her home. And yet she was glad he was there.

"No. Not at all. Just lying here thinking." He reached for the remote and shutoff the TV. "Mindless stuff," he said.

"We don't watch much anymore. Just old movies, and
dad, uh George, well he likes football. The two chairs in the room were covered with old clothing she had recently gathered for a local Big Brothers/ Big Sisters clothing drive. There was no place to sit. Harold patted the quilted bed cover.

"Sit down," he said. She did.

"How are you, Harold?" He looked quizzically at her. He liked her, but during the divorce she was anything but friendly. That was understandable. He had tried to make it as amenable as possible, but it was still a wrenching apart, complicated by David's anger and fear.

"I'm okay, Carol. More important, how are you? I mean about tonight, and with Jen's thing, and all that?" Carol took his measure, plumbing the depth of Harold's sincerity through his eyes. She decided that she was comfortable answering.

Oh? I'm okay. I think George was right. It was time for Christmas again. And, as you call it, 'Jen's thing', well...we'll know more about it on Monday and take it from there. But she is my child, so her pain and suffering is also mine. You have a son. You know what I mean." He nodded his agreement. "What are your plans?" she asked directly.

"About what?"

"About Jenny. I see how you are toward her."

"I still love her. And of course I love David."

"Love isn't a plan, Harold."

"I know. But I just had to be with them tonight... now. I couldn't stay away."

"For you or for them?"

"Probably both."

"I want you to think about what you're doing. You're a grown man. Jenny's going through her own private Hell now. She's afraid not just for herself, but for David. And he's scared that she is going to die." Carol's eyes watered a bit, but she quickly brushed the tears away. This wasn't about her. "I believe that beating this 'thing', if the tests come back the way they might, depends on Jenny's state of mind and her will to fight. She needs support with no distractions. If you think you want to try to, well, patch things up in some way, I want you to be sure..."

"I understand mom," he said.

"Because you may not get another chance, Harold."

"Yes," was all he could muster. After she left the room he turned his face into the pillow and wept.

CHAPTER EIGHTEEN

PLACES OF MEMORY

When George and Matthew returned to the house Carol was standing at the foot of the staircase with fresh bedding in her arms.

"Jenny and family are in for the night," she said to George. "I'm not really up to church tonight, are you?"

"No," George answered. He turned to Matthew. "If you want to go to church tonight you're welcome to take the truck. You know where the church is, right?"

"Yes. But I don't thinks so," Matthew said. "I'm pretty bushed. I've been on the road since before dawn."

"Right. I forgot," George remarked, smiling. "Funny... It feels like you've been here for more than just tonight."

The tow men went upstairs, quietly following Carol down the corridor. George stopped at Jennifer's room and peeked inside for a moment, then carefully closed it.

"They're both fast asleep," he told Carol. "David had a smile on his face."

"Visions of sugar plums," Matthew whispered. Carol was pleased with that image.

"Thank God," she said. They reached a closed door and she stopped. "I thought we'd put Matthew in, uh here..."

"Exactly my thought," George agreed, before she had finished. He opened the door to John's room and turned on the overhead light. Carol paused and took a deep breath. She went in. Matthew followed. It was a modestly sized room – no more than fifteen by fifteen. Framed photographs covered three walls. Sport trophies cluttered the top of a four drawer, Early American, walnut dresser. A single bed, against the far wall was covered by a faded blue chenille spread. The headboard was also walnut, but a darker tone than the dresser. A lone window to the left of the bed looked out on the barn and the fields beyond.

Carol stripped off the spread and began to make up the bed with the sheet, pillowcase, and comforter she had brought up from the linen closets. George helped her while Matthew studied the room.

"This was John's room," George said as he stuffed two pillows into dark blue pillowcases. "We kept some of his things here. The rest are in the attic."

"I figured that," Matthew said. He put his bag down. The two men stood silent, looking at the pictures, as Carol finished making the bed. She moved two of the larger trophies aside and placed a bath towel and washcloth on the dresser. She was done preparing the room for their guest.

"Well," George said as he stretched, "I need a hot shower and a soft welcoming bed. Good-night, Matthew. Sleep well. I'll see you in the morning."

"Good-night, George. And thank again for having me here. Merry Christmas."

"Merry Christmas to you too." George left. Carol remained, gazing around the room, wistfully.

"Well...here you are," she said quietly. "The bathroom is right next door. Harold is asleep, and we have our own, so feel free."

"Thanks... Thanks for everything, Mrs. Boyajian."

"Carol. I...we've been grateful for your being part of this Christmas." She walked to the door. "Matthew..." she said. pausing at the door. "I want to say something. I hope you'll understand. When I was a child, I had a small glass globe. You know - the kind that you can shake and it snows?" He nodded. "My Nana, Grandma, gave it to me. I loved it. I used to play a game. I'd shake it and then wish for something before the flakes settled to the bottom. Well... Today, and tonight, when it snowed? It felt like I had that globe in my hands again, except I was inside, and it was the whole world. My whole world."

"A beautiful world," he said softly.

"Yes... So I made a wish -a magical, impossible wish. And somehow, with all that's happened tonight, I think it might have come true." Their eyes met, each unable to turn away.

"Sure. Why not?" Matthew said. "It's Christmas. But remember that those kid of wishes must always be kept close to the heart, and secret."

"Yes... I thought you'd say something like that." He stepped closer to her.

"I want you that its been wonderful they way you all have welcomed me into your home. Especially tonight, at such a difficult time for you. It was..."

"Perfect that you are here!" she interrupted. If they spoke much longer she felt she might burst into tears. Whether they were tears of joy, or sorrow, she did not know. "Merry Christmas Matthew, whoever you are... And Godspeed to wherever it is that you're going." She quickly left, closing the door softly behind her. Out in the hall, she whispered she leaned against the door and looked up toward Heaven. "Good-night, son...wherever you are. And a very Merry Christmas." Her words warmed her soul. She felt John had heard them.

Matthew stared at the door for a moment then slowly turned in a circle, examining the room more carefully. His gaze fell upon the State Championship Baseball Trophy, and then on a baseball bat leaning against the wall in the corner of the room. He picked it up and assumed a batter's stance.

"Bases loaded. Down three – zip. Two out. State Championship on the line. Three balls - two strikes. It all comes down to this. Here it is... Heat. Right down the middle," Matthew pantomimed a slow motion swing at the pitch. He made a loud clicking sound with his tongue, mimicking the sound of the bat connecting with the ball. "And there it goes, folks... Out of the ballpark!" He smiled, pleased with his imagined home run. He then put the bat aside. On the wall, next to the High School baseball team picture, he studied a photograph of John in fatigues, kicking back with his squad in Saudi Arabia. He then glanced back at the team photograph.

"Two different worlds. Two different people," he muttered to himself. Matthew took the picture from the wall, and cradled it in his trembling hands like a holy man might hold a sacred book.

"Ahhhh," he sighed. "Ahhhh, John. They didn't know you, did they? You were just getting to know yourself." Matthew sat down on the on the edge of the bed.

"You couldn't hear their words of love... 'Be safe. Be smart. Take care.' No. Heart pounding. Drums beating. Blood running hot. Trumpets of glory... Of glory... It was all the glory of youth..." He held the photo against his chest.

He could hear the throttling rhythm of machine gun fire. Mortars exploding, taking the measure of his position. Above and behind, the panicked shouts above the helicopter's whirring blades. Within the dry, dusty, cloud, raised by liftoff, streaking tails of out-going red tracers - and incoming green tracers illuminated the barren, pockmarked, landscape. White and yellowish light, as the exploding mortar rounds silhouetted twisted, dark shapes of the enemy as they closed, smelling blood and victory in the insane ballet of war.

The images passed out of his consciousness. He rose and walked to the window. The wind had picked up, blowing powdery snow in lacy swirls across the field. The moon glowed brightly, but was moving toward the horizon. Silent night. Holy night. He could see tracks left by the deer, and then a second set of tracks trailing behind them off into the night. Seekers?   Predators? How many, he wondered. How many didn't make it home for Christmas?

Matthew draped his jacket on the back of a cane chair, the only other piece of furniture in the room. He removed his shirt, boots, socks, trousers, and T-shirt. His arms, legs, shoulders, back, chest, neck and torso were covered with dark, mean, purple scars – the fleshy marks of war and life that man inflicts on man. He took no notice of them. He knew each personally. Matthew turned off the small lamp on the dresser. He lay down on the bed in his shorts, propping a pillow beneath his head. He stared up at the ceiling, and through it, out into the starry night, and beyond into endless space. Then he closed his eyes and there was only darkness and peace.

CHAPTER NINETEEN

IN DREAMS

Jennifer slept soundly beneath her soft, down comforter. David, wrapped in two blankets on the cot near the far wall, also enjoyed a deep sleep. A vivid, emotional dream grew her Jenny, bathing her senses like a warm summer rain.

Her brother John, seventeen, was at the wheel of a 1960 cream-puff Chevrolet Impala that he and daddy had lovingly restored. Eight-year-old Jennifer bounced with excitement in the passenger seat next to him.

"This is soooo great, Johnny. Your very own car! Can we get some ice cream?"

"Sure, kiddo."

"Wait 'til my friends see me."

"Hey. You know what? You're my first date in the new wheels..." Jennifer squealed with joy. But then the road abruptly began to glow brighter on John's side, while darkening on Jennifer's. They were suddenly moving through two different worlds,

hurtling along like a train on distinctly different tracks.

"What is it, Johnny?"

"Don't worry, Jenny. Nothing to be afraid of." Then the Chevy divided. The halves split and veered off away from one another. One carried John into the light, the other pulled Jennifer into darkness.

"Johnnie? What's happening?" she shouted in panic to her brother.

"Good-bye Jennifer!" he answered, waving once and then disappearing into the blinding, glowing light.

"Johnny!" she screamed. "No! Johnny wait... Please don't! Wait!"

Jennifer opened her eyes. Her nightgown was soaked with sweat. Shaken, the powerful reality of her dream remained with her. She tossed the blanket aside and got out of bed, shivering and burning up at the same time. John's disappearing image was still before her eyes. Had she screamed out in her sleep? She glanced at David. No. He was sound asleep. She crossed the room to a pair of French Doors that opened onto a small balcony. The moonlit snowscape spread out before her. Although she wore no slippers she did not feel the snow on her bare feet as she stood there. She breathed in deeply. Unconsciously, she slid her right hand slowly up to her breasts, caressing them firmly. Astonished, she stopped in mid-breath and gasped. Her eyes widened. She looked down at her hand in wonderment.

George, in a deep sleep, shifted restlessly on his side in bed. His head tossed from side to side.

A much younger George and John were busy together at the workbench. John was using a miter and saw while George guided his son's hands. Young John's face was serious and intense as he concentrated on the task.

"Keep your eye on the saw," George coached him. "Remember to use even, steady, straight strokes." John looked at his father. "Are you ready?" John nodded and clenched his teeth. "Let her rip." John was determined as he pushed and pulled the saw. With each stroke his tongue flicked in and out between his lips. Filled with pride, George watched his son work. The length of framing was sawed through. George took it to another bench and fit it together with other pieces of a frame. It was a perfect match. "Good job, son. You've got magic

in your hands."

"Like you dad?"

"You bet. We're a team."

"A team. Yeah...We'll always be a team, won't we?"

Suddenly the frame on the workbench shattered sending fragments in every direction. George ducked to avoid them, but John did not. The wood became hot metal that tore into his flesh, and took away his son's youth, and his life. No matter how he tried to help John, he could as his son's body was ravaged and destroyed.

George flailed and awoke. He immediately sat up and shook his hear to drive away the awful dream. It took a few moments to realize that Carol was not in bed next to him. Then he heard voices, excited whispers, coming from down the hallway. He got up, grabbed his robe, and followed the sound to Jennifer's room. The room was freezing. Jennifer's bed was empty. The French Doors were ajar. David was fast asleep. He tucked the blankets around his grandson. The whispers were coming from the balcony where he found Carol and Jennifer standing barefoot and ankle-deep in snow.

"Hey girls... What's going on? You're gonna'

catch your death out here." Jennifer turned and embraced her father.

"Oh daddy! It's a miracle!" George held his daughter, who was trembling in his arms, and looked questioningly at Carol. She was grinning and wiping tears from her cheeks. All she could do was nod and smile - wide and joyful.

"It is George. A miracle for sure!" Carol told him.

"Okay," he said, starting to shiver. "Come inside and tell me. But keep it down. David's still sleeping."

They quietly made their way down to the kitchen. Jennifer held onto her father as tightly as she ever had. Carol walked ahead of them, lightly on her feet, like a ballet dance about to perform a giant leap of joy. The moonlight was so bright in the kitchen that no other light was needed. George closed the kitchen door. Jennifer could not contain her excitement.

"Oh daddy. It's incredible. Mom and I... We had this dream," Jennifer began, "A dream about Johnny."

"Not the same dream," Carol added.

"No. Not the same."

"Mine was calm," Carol said. "I was here... In this very kitchen preparing dinner and Johnny came in. You remember when he was ten and played in Little League?" George nodded, trying to be patient as he wondered what all this had to do with a miracle. "Well..." Carol continued, "He came in with a bouquet of wild spring flowers tucked behind his back and handed them to me." She wiped a tear away. "He told me that I was his best girl." Her voice cracked. "That I would always be his best girl." The tears flowed and she could speak no more.

"I had a dream about John, too," George said, noting his wife's emotion.

"You did!" Both women said in unison.

"Yes. I guess we're all thinking about him in our own personal way tonight."

"Because we're having Christmas again," Carol said.

"Or maybe because Matthew is here and talked about Johnny," Jennifer said quietly.

"So stop the torture," George finally said. "What, in the name of God, is this miracle?" Jennifer moved to her father. She opened her nightgown and showed him her breast where the lumpectomy had been performed.

"Here is it... Or rather, here it isn't!" There was

no bandage. There was no scar. There was nothing but smooth, firm skin.

"And I have no pain, daddy. No scar. There's nothing. It's gone!   I don't need stitches out on Monday, or any test results. I'm cured!" George put his hand to his mouth as if to block a shout of joy. His breath rushed through his fingers.

"Dear Lord," he said. "Oh my dear Lord..."

At that moment a gust of wind rattled against the kitchen window. It seemed to beckoned them. As the three looked out, their arms entwined, a halo surrounded the setting moon. Beyond the barn, across the snowy field, standing near the edge of the woods was Matthew. The wind stirred wisps of snow around him, like feathers drifting down from a flock of Great White Egrets. As the snow swirled and settled they could see that Matthew was with the small herd of deer, and three large, silver-gray wolves. He moved among them, pausing before each creature to stroke it lovingly. The group then walked peacefully across the field – predator and prey, at peace. The animals left no tracks in the snow. Neither did Matthew.

CHAPTER TWENTY

A CHRISTMAS MORNING PROMISE

At first light, David sat up in bed. His heart was pounding with excitement. He was careful to be quiet as he put on his jeans and bulky knit Irish sweater that Grandma had given him to wear yesterday. It had belonged to Uncle John, and he felt very proud to wear it. He paused for a moment and looked at his mother, who was enjoying a deep, restful sleep. She seemed somehow different to him; younger. He skin was glowing. Her peaceful vision made David smile. He loved her very much.

It was warm in the room. David stepped out into the hallway. He slipped on his sneakers without socks. The guest room door was closed. Grandma and Grandpa's door was also closed. The door to Uncle John's room was open. David peeked inside, but no one was there. The bed had not been slept in. David wondered where Matthew had slept. He hoped the visitor had not left without saying good-bye. He liked Matthew and he knew the feeling was mutual. David also hoped that Matthew had more stories about Uncle John to tell him.

The lights on the Christmas tree illuminated the bottom of the stairs in soft, glowing spurts of red, green, white, and blue as it spilled out of the living room. The colors filled David with excitement and anticipation. He hopped down the last few steps and rushed into the living room. There, under the tree, was a pile of gifts. Four were neatly wrapped in red and green paper, tied with large red bows. Three others had Santa and his elves paper, tied with white ribbon. And there were others with blue and silver paper; one with bright red foil. Next to the fireplace was a large mesh stocking filled with a wonderful assortment of toys, games, and candy. David rushed to the tree and attacked the largest box that he could not lift. A large tag, with bold lettering, read 'For David – Merry Christmas from Mommy and Daddy'. He tore at the wrapping paper like an eager puppy digging up a favorite bone. He threw the paper aside and stared at the picture on the box. A two-wheeler bicycle! Red and white - with a horn and a light and three gears?

"That's a beauty," a voice behind him said. Matthew sat in shadows in the wing chair near the fireplace. David spun around beaming.

"Yeah! Matthew. I thought maybe you left without saying good-bye." Matthew got up. He was dressed. His B-4 bag, with his jacket draped over it, lay on the floor next to him.

"That would never happen, David," he said. He walked over to the tree. "That is some super bike. I always wanted one like it when I was a kid. It looks like you have lots of presents." David glanced at all the boxes under and around the tree.

"This is the best Christmas!" He looked at the presents again. "But I don't see any for you," David said sadly.

"Don't you worry. I'll get mine later, when I get to where I'm going."

"Do you have to go?" David stood up.

"Yes." David put his head down and turned away. Matthew put his arm around the boy.

"Hey there, pal. Cheer up. If I could stay, I surely would. But I can't. I have another place to be. And you have Christmas with your family. That's the best." David looked up at Matthew.

"But I really like you, Matthew. You're like my friend."

"I am your friend and I'm really happy that I got to meet you." He knelt down next to David. "I want you to do me a favor."

"What?"

"You make sure that you spend every Christmas you can with your family. And every day you can, tell them that you love them. Will you do that?"

David smiled.

"Sure. That's easy. Because I do love them." David then reached out and hugged Matthew as hard as he had ever hugged anyone before. "I love you too." Matthew put his arms around the boy and held him close.

"Yes, David..." he said softly to the boy. "Me too." He let David go. "Now let's see what else Santa brought for you..."

A half-hour later George and Carol, in their bathrobes, stepped from their bedroom into the hallway. They checked, in Jennifer's room, but no one was there. The door to John's room was ajar, but the room was also empty.

"They must all be downstairs," Carol said. With that the door to the guest room opened and Jennifer and Harold came out. They were holding hands. Jennifer had told Harold what had happened, and had shown him the physical proof of healing. When he saw that her bandage and scar were gone, he'd wept. She had held him in her arms and in the spirit that pervaded this home, she forgave him.

"I love you," she had told him, plain and simple.

"And I you, Jen. I'm so very sorry for being such an insensitive jerk. I really am." She did not answer, but stroked his hair, and patted his back, and held him close against her strong, healthy body. Each knew they would reconcile and that their lives and love for one another was a great gift, worth fighting for a preserving from this day forward.

A squeal of joy drifted up from downstairs as the people upstairs stood in the hallway.

"Someone's into his presents," George said.

"He sounds so happy," Harold said.

"As we all are," Jennifer added, squeezing his hand. "Let's go see..."

"Just a sec," George said. "Are we still agreed about Matthew?" After experiencing what they had seen last night, George, Carol, and Jennifer decided they would say nothing about it to Matthew. 'Let him tell us,' George had suggested. 'If he wants to...' They were all sure that what they had witnessed, and what had happened to Jenny, was somehow connected, and miraculous. They didn't quite know how to deal with it.

"Why don't we just experience the uplifting euphoria of all this," Carol had suggested, "And accept the gift with gratitude and love?" They all agreed.

When the family came downstairs they found the living room cluttered with wrapping paper. Most of David's gifts were open. Every game and toy was assembled and functioning. Every bit of clothing had been tried on. The centerpiece of David's happiness, his new bike was assembled. It's shiny silver and blue metallic frame reflected the lights from the tree. David was astride it and pedaling furiously as Matthew held the rear wheel up off the floor.

"Mommy, Daddy, Grandma, Grandpa! Look! Matthew put it together." The look on David's face said it all. Christmas had once again arrived in the Boyajian home.

CHAPTER TWENTY-ONE

FAREWELL IS NOT GOOD-BYE

Carol offered to make breakfast, but Matthew declined.

"All I usually have is coffee. An old habit."

"Not even some toast?"

"No thank you. My ride will be at the Interstate in half an hour. I don't want to miss it." They all were struggling with so many unanswered questions, and the frustration of having no time to ask, to talk, to learn the truth.

"Please? Stay for one more night," Jennifer begged.

"I would love to, but I can't. My ride...It's arranged. I'm sorry." Matthew slipped on his jacket. He turned to George. "I think we should be going." George nodded. Matthew picked up his bag. Matthew headed for the front door, followed by Jennifer and Harold, who was holding David's hand. They were followed by Carol whose arm was entwined in George's. They walked down the now shoveled path slowly, in single file, ceremonially.

It was a bright, sunny, winter morning. A spectacular White Christmas - the kind that makes you squint from the glare bouncing off fresh, white snow. The bare, deciduous, tree limbs were coated with snow, like vanilla frosting on a coral reef. The conifers, mostly silver spruce and cedar, stood tall, bearing the weight of the snow on their broad green shoulders. There was a gusty breeze that blew glistening wisps of snow across the path, and swirled sparkling flakes around in the field beyond. The landscape was silent, surreal, and magical in the clear morning air as though a great hand had cleansed the earth to welcome Christmas Day.

They all gathered awkwardly next to the pickup. Carol and Jennifer stood on either side of Matthew, his B-4 bag slung over his shoulder. Sensing the women wanted a private moment, George signaled to Harold who took David by the hand and went around to the driver's door. Jennifer's mind raced, seeking the right words.

"If I could stay, I would," Matthew said, easing the moment. "I surely would."

"I believe you," Jennifer replied. "I just don't know how to..."

"You already have," he answered.

"I have?"

"By sharing Christmas with me. By opening your home and your hearts you gave me a place to rest and fill my soul with peace." Jennifer could say no more. Choked with emotion she reached up and embraced Matthew with her arms around his neck. "Thank you," she whispered in his ear. "Thank you with all my heart." She stepped away. He was smiling.

"You know you're always welcome..." Carol's voice trailed off. She knew she would never have the answers she craved, but somehow it didn't matter right now.

"Yes, I do. You have a wonderful home here... a family... a good life. Hold it close... Keep it safe... Always."

"It's Christmas," she said as she took his hand in hers. You came so suddenly to us. I had no time... to buy you a...to get you a Christmas present. And you gave us... So much..."

"Presents don't make Christmas. Love does."

Carol
Nodded and stroked his face. Then she gently kissed him on the cheek.

"But I do have something for you." She reached

into her apron pocket and removed the engraved watch that Elizabeth had given her yesterday. She handed it to Matthew. "This is for you."

"Thank you," said Matthew. He did not protest, but looked at the watch for a brief moment, then nodded and slipped it into his pocket. "I am honored." She embraced him one last time and whispered, "God bless you." Her eyes filled with tears. Joyful tears. Carol stepped back and adjusted his jacket collar in a tender, motherly, way.

"Merry Christmas," he said to both women, then walked to the truck. George got in his other side as Harold and David came around to say their good-bye. Harold shook Matthew's hand. Although neither wore gloves, and the temperature was well below freezing, Matthew's touch was again as warm as it had been when they met last night.

"It was good to meet you, Matthew. I am...we are all grateful. Really grateful."

"Yes. Me too. You take good care of your family," Matthew said. He put his hand on David's head. The boy stared down at the snow, unwilling to say good-bye. "Remember what I asked you today, David. Okay?" David looked up at Matthew.

"Okay," was all he could muster. He reached out and hugged Matthew around the waist.

"Now have a Merry Christmas." Matthew picked up his bag and got into the truck. George started the engine. He backed up and turned down the driveway toward the road. Carol and Jennifer, standing arm in arm in the bright, morning light, waved. Harold picked David up so he better see into the truck. Matthew waved back, and then, as George turned onto the road, he was gone.

CHAPTER TWENTY-TWO

TRUTH REVEALED

George and Matthew drove in silence until they approached the place on the road where they had first met yesterday afternoon. George looked at his watch. Nearly eight o'clock. He could no longer hold back. The words came pouring out, fast and breathless.

"Last night... There was so much you knew about John...things we didn't discuss. And Jennifer. She's healed. The dreams we had. We saw you in the field..." Matthew raised his hand, palm toward George, and shook his head 'no' as if asking him not to speak. "Please..." George could not help himself. They reached the exact spot where George had nearly hit Matthew. "There's so much we need to know..."

"You can let me off here," Matthew said softly.

"Here?" He was confused. "But you said the Interstate was where..."

"This'll be just fine." There was finality in Matthew's voice that could not be denied. George pulled the pickup over to the side of the road. He looked at Matthew to speak, but the younger man was already half out the door. The two men, lone figures on the snowy landscape, got out their respective sides and walked around to the rear of the truck. They stood eye to eye, man to man.

"I don't know what all this means. But I do know that you have made our Christmas... You've helped make our lives whole again, and for that we will be eternally grateful," George said.

"It's time," the visitor said. "I've got to go." He started to walk away. George followed.

"But... Go where? Please..." Matthew stopped and smiled warmly. He shook the older man's hand.

"This is how it has to be." He then let go of George's hand. Suddenly, the wind came up and grew strong. A gust blew a flurry of snow off the field next to the road. It pushed George back toward the truck and blinded him momentarily. Unwilling to be moved, he fought the force. Then the wind died as suddenly as it had begun. Through a mist of sparkling, swirling, snow, he saw Matthew raise his hand in a military salute. George's hand automatically rose to the peak of his cap and he returned the salute. Then another, stronger gust blew and snow swirled around Matthew, obliterating

George's view of him. When the wind stopped and the snow settled the thirty-five year old Matthew had been replaced by a John. He wore his Army dress greens, polished black jump boots, and a chest full of the medals and ribbons – the same as those that George had kept in his workshop. It was a young, proud, John Boyajian who now saluted his father. And then wind gusted again and swirled, churning up more of the crystalline flakes. When it cleared, John was gone. George ran to the spot where a moment before he had seen his son. There were footprints leading from the road into the field beyond where they ended. Only the pristine snow lay beyond, and the woods. The wind was only a soft whisper, and then there was silence.

"Merry Christmas, son," George finally spoke out into the clear, still, morning air. Then he heard that unmistakable voice.

"Merry Christmas, dad. Keep it always. And remember I love you." George knelt and touched the last footprint, now filling with fresh blowing snow. Soon it would be gone, like his only son. Then George noticed something next to the vanishing footprint. He cleared away the snow. There, underneath, he found Elizabeth's watch – the one she had bought for John...the one that Carol had given to Matthew earlier. George held it up in the sunlight and read the inscription. 'Home for Christmas – Love Always, Lizzie and John'.

George waited at the spot until the blowing snow finally filled in all the footprints. And then, with the vision, touch and voice of his son locked forever in his heart, he walked to the truck and drove home to his wife and family to always celebrate Christmas.